THE SOLDIER

SERVE IN HEAVEN...
Or Reign in Hell...

A Series Novel

D'QUBE

The Soldier: SERVE IN HEAVEN...
Or Reign in Hell...
Copyright © 2023 by D'Qube

ISBN:

Paperback: 978-1959151593

e-book: 978-1959151609

The Reading Glass Books
1-888-420-3050
www.readingglassbooks.com
production@readingglassbooks.com

Contents

Prologue

Rapture has come. He knew the time was near. He lost his wife, his children. It was just him. He was caught between faith and self-preservation. He walked along the streets of Denmark. His body was cold with anguish and pain. He had no sense of purpose at that time—a loner looking for answers. He was searching for purpose or direction.

"God, what is it you want of me?" No answer. He turned up his collar and proceeded down the street. The weather was cool and breezy. His thoughts, like the breeze in the air, flurried through his mind switching from one topic to another. A brisk breeze nudged his neck to remind him the winter chill was still prevalent. He turned up his collar as he walked toward the people in the street. They were caught up in their busy lives, consumed with surviving. The universal code was taking its toll. Anyone who was familiar with Revelations knew what the "code" was—three "sixes." But this was not your common mark that was so easy to distinguish; it was an implanted tattoo-like marking that could be read via scanner prior to making purchases.

People knew survival was not possible unless you submitted to the "code." Those that knew better found other ways to survive. Adrian was one of those who chose a different method. He continued down the street focused on multiple questions flashing through his head like a broken projector. He knew the deal he had made and was intent on keeping it. Adrian walked several blocks as he weaved through crowds and traffic, navigating through the organized chaos in the city. Hunger had distracted his thoughts, and luckily for him, a few yards away was a local fruit stand located in the town square.

He patiently waited in the short line of customers making their purchases. When it was his turn, the merchant looked at him, frowned, and turned away. There was an assortment of items on his makeshift cart—plums, apples, figs, nectarines, some of which seemingly out of character for the season, all ripe and sultry to the eye as well as to his hunger. Adrian picked up a plum, its soft texture resonated a rich dark purple hue that begged to be devoured. He tried to make eye contact with the merchant who was doing his best to seem distracted.

"How much?"

The salesman pretended not to hear him.

Adrian thought to himself, *Ahh, hell, here we go.*

"I said how much?"

The salesman looked at him with disgust.

"I don't serve niggers!"

"Good, because I don't cater to any either. Now like I said before... how much?"

"Listen, boy, didn't you understand me? I don't serve your kind. Now I suggest you leave... or else—"

"Or else what?" Adrian barked.

"Or else this world will be minus one nigger," he stated as he raised his shirt up to expose the butt of a revolver he had neatly tucked in his waistband.

Adrian smiled as he placed the plum down and reached for a nectarine. The salesman grabbed a knife he had on the counter and pierced Adrian's hand. The blade protruded to the opposite end. Adrian just smiled and ate the nectarine with his other hand. The smile slowly faded as he turned and looked at the salesman.

"You will die from the same hate you have for me." Adrian spoke with a low and ominous voice.

The salesman looked at Adrian and reached for his gun, but it was too late. Adrian's eyes turned blood red. His stare became as cold as death. The salesman's body trembled violently, his eyes matching the blood red color of Adrian's. Shortly there was a loud pop as the salesman's heart exploded. His body crumbled to the ground. Blood spewed from every opening of his body. Adrian reached in his pocket and pulled out a single gold coin. He left the currency on the counter and grabbed another piece of fruit as he walked away. He had walked a good distance when he realized the knife was still in his hand. He closed his eyes and inhaled. With one pull, he removed the knife from his hand. He looked at the knife and its craftsmanship. The handle was a dark leather almost a black hue with leather rolled straps that neatly wrapped around the handle like a tightly coiled snaked nested upon its grip.

The blade shined like a brand-new nickel fresh from a mint. Despite a few specks of blood on the blade, it looked beautiful.

"Nice knife."

He threw it on the ground as his body mended the injury almost instantly. He thought about his action briefly as he proceeded to his destination—whether or not he was justified in killing the clerk or discarding of the knife so carelessly.

After some mental argument with himself, he finally decided it was both.

The cold nipped at his naked neck like tiny stings that engulfed his senses with no mercy. He pulled the collar of his jacket up to barricade the unforgiving wind, as he walked to the hotel located a few blocks down. Within minutes, he had arrived; Waldorf Astoria Amsterdam stared back at him with grander and beauty. The entrance looked pricey with its unique statues that adorned the outside of the door guarding the contents from unworthy sorts. The auto revolving door traced a deep velvet red carpet that surrounded the circled doorway. The lobby oozed of elegance and sophistication. Each décor announced the years of prestige of the hotel. Small Greek figurines strategically scattered themselves throughout the room.

Bellboys scuffled through greeting as many guests as they could to provide the hotel's signature customer service. Some grabbed bags eagerly as they waited patiently for the customer to complete the check in process. Adrian, still veering from the incident earlier, showed little patience as he walked to the counter.

"Yes, sir, may I help you?" the female clerk asked.

"Yes, I need a room for tonight."

"Do you wish to use the code?"

"No, I'll use this." He pulled out three gold coins from his pocket and laid them on the counter. The clerk smiled and handed him his key.

"God be with you," she whispered so as not to promote any attention from passersby.

Adrian smiled because he knew that greeting. She was aware of his purpose. He grabbed her hand, as if to say, "Stay faithful." She smiled nodding her head, quickly released his hand, and turned away. He knew he could not draw too much attention for fear of execution. Besides, she was not given the same abilities he had.

The lady politely motioned for the bellboy as Adrian politely declined the offer. He maneuvered through the small crowd of people who had gathered toward the center of the hotel floor to the elevator. He was a little deterred they would just block the flow of traffic as they marveled over the hotel's décor. He hit the "up" button and entered the elevator.

The doors opened just as graceful as the ambiance that filled the atmosphere of the hotel. He stepped inside and playfully punched the number pad for the second floor to get to the room he was assigned. The elevator door closed as gracefully as it opened. There was a slight jerk as the elevator hurriedly hurled itself to the second floor. There was a soft computer-generated voice that announced his arrival.

"Floor two."

As if on command, the doors opened gracefully once more. Adrian used the wall signs to navigate to his designated room. Seconds later, he found his room 223; he placed the electronic card key into the designated slot as the green indicator lit in approval to grant access to his room. He marveled at the design of the room. A large king-sized bed was positioned regally against the accent wall. The dark green color promoted its dominance against the soft cream-colored walls that surrounded the rest of the room. The beautiful thick comforter shielded the large bed from any foreign intrusion.

Its warm soft forest green with tannish patterned accents complemented the accent wall, body pillows of various green and white lay across the head of the bed. A large wooden desk set off to the right of the bed. The dark cherry wood shined from the polish that was evidently done earlier. A notepad sat neatly on the desk with two executive pens on either side. A Cisco phone sat on the desk as the lightly lit display showed the room number. Directly ten feet from the bed sat an entertainment center that host a large 40" Sony Smart TV, a mini-bar, and a DVR receiver that seemed ready to honor the guests' viewing pleasure. There was a small divider wall that separated the main room from the bath and closet. A small vanity was tucked neatly alongside its inside interior as the mirrored closet mocked its image of both he and the vanity.

He opened the door leading to the bath; inside was an executive shower with a whirlpool bath and a toilet that was too immaculate to use. Adrian pleased with his accommodations, removed his jacket, and lay across the bed.

His body felt cold but burning at the same time. He heard the sirens scream in distress in the background. He knew why.

They finally noticed the salesman's body near the fruit stand. He closed his eyes as his body slumped into a deep relaxed state. Within seconds, Adrian was asleep.

"Why did you kill him?"

"I didn't, his hate killed him."

"Vengeance is mine, said the Lord."

"It was not vengeance, it was principle."

Adrian's body tensed up; his entire body felt like he was burning from the inside out. The sensation resided as he felt cold and feverish.

"I have been sent to give you more. Practice forgiveness and you will experience restraint. Time is of the essence you cannot be exposed... practice restraint."

Adrian awoke with a jerk. He was cold, but his bed was drenched with sweat. He looked around trying to distinguish dream from reality.

His chest hurt something awful as he rubbed the source of the pain. He noticed a mark on his chest that slowly faded away.

Adrian got out of bed and walked sluggishly to the bathroom. He was still cold, but he felt like his body was on fire. He glared into the mirror as he searched for the mark on his chest, but it was gone. Caught in a daze, he reluctantly looked at his watch and noticed it was 9 a.m.

"Wow, I really was tired," he thought to himself. He realized he had slept the entire day away. Adrian didn't bother to shower as he knew he did not have time to waste. His stomach was talking to his back, and he knew what that meant. It was time to eat.

The dream he had prior seemed to haunt his thoughts. He could not argue the fact that it was revenge for the way the clerk treated him. He thought to himself that he was wrong, and he knew the clerk was at an unfair advantage. Two wrongs don't make a right, as the old saying goes. He put his shirt on, grabbed his jacket and room key, and proceeded to the elevator. He hit the "down" button as he patiently waited for his motored carriage to arrive. The elevator dinged as it slowly settled on his floor. He entered the elevator as the doors slowly and gracefully closed as if to protect its precious cargo. There was a slight pause in speed as it gently rested on the first floor. The doors once again gently opened and allowed its cargo to exit safely.

Adrian rounded the corner to spot the hotel's restaurant. He walked in and patiently waited to be seated. A petite woman who looked no older than twenty or so greeted him with a warm and welcoming smile.

"Table for one?" she asked.

"Yes, please," Adrian answered.

The woman briskly walked toward the nearest table with Adrian in tow.

"Is this fine?" the woman asked.

"This is fine, thank you."

The woman laid the silverware neatly on the table along with the menu she had in her possession earlier.

"Your server will be with you shortly."

Adrian thanked the hostess and began to browse through the menu. He viewed the choices with dismay. It wasn't home. He missed shrimp and grits, biscuits and gravy, ham steak and cane syrup.

A voice startled him and rudely destroyed his reminisce of his Southern upbringing.

"Hello, my name is Josh, I will be your server today, and may I start you off with something to drink?"

He was a tall rather slim gentleman in his early to mid-twenties. His nicely pressed slacks held a slight crease as his crisp button-downed shirt displayed its professional and customer-oriented persona. Adrian chuckled under his breath.

Josh needs to eat some of what he grew up on to put some meat on his bones, he thought.

"Coffee for now please, thank you."

Josh nodded his head and walked away to retrieve his order. Adrian, on the other hand, sat in a state of indecisiveness. Nothing he saw was appealing. Homesick and flustered, he went the only route he knew how to satisfy his Southern craving. On the menu was oatmeal and fruit, can't mess that up, and to put a band-aid on his craving, he figured he would have bacon and toast added. Josh returned with his coffee and dutifully placed it on the table. He also placed in front of Adrian a small serving of cream and a container of various sugars and sweeteners.

"Are you ready to order, sir?"

"Yes, I would like a bowl of oatmeal, two slices of toast grilled please, two slices of bacon, and some fruit please."

Josh nodded as he did before and retrieved the menu from Adrian. As Josh walked away, Adrian pulled his phone from his jacket pocket. He logged into his phone and launched the email app to see what he had missed. Thirty-seven missed emails. He scrolled through emails he felt were important to view and deleted the remainder. He minimized the app and opened his Chrome browser. He typed in "MSN.com" to catch the news he had missed due to his long slumber. The news had not changed much; as usual, it was much of the same. Depressing. Engulfed in a few articles, he was abruptly interrupted by Josh.

"Excuse me, sir, here is your meal."

Adrian gave a forgiving smile as he prepared to eat his makeshift Southern substitute breakfast. He devoured his meal as if he had not eaten in months. Everything was delicious even his lukewarm coffee he had left unattended. Josh revisited the table and asked if Adrian needed anything else.

"No, I'm fine, thank you."

Josh smiled and placed the check on the table.

"Whenever you're ready, sir."

Adrian placed on the check two gold coins more than the amount on the check.

"Keep the change." Adrian smiled.

Josh returned a gracious smile. "Thank you, sir!"

Adrian left the restaurant and walked to the front desk. He removed the room key from his coat and placed it on the counter. There was a new clerk at the desk. Not as nice. He stood with a snobbish demeanor.

His sandy blond hair neatly tapered around his semi-round head. He was dressed in a nicely tailored Giorgio Armani suit. He sarcastically barked his commands at the staff as if they were beneath him. His arrogance exuded from him like a foul order. Adrian knew there would be a problem as he patiently waited until he barked his last insulting command to his subordinates.

As if on cue, he swung his head toward Adrian's direction.

"Are you checking out?" the clerk asked in a condescending tone.

"Yes."

The clerk rolled his eyes. "They'll let anyone sleep in this God-forsaken place."

Adrian smiled as his insides burned with contentment and disdain for the clerk and his snide comment. "Lucky for you I am practicing restraint, muthafucker. Have a good day."

The clerk was in shock from the return comment. At a loss for words, he turned and darted into the back office. Adrian walked out of the door, turned up his collar, and preceded down the street. He thought about the dream and what he had done to the salesman. He could not argue.

It was vengeance. *Man has so much to atone for*, he thought. He was halfway to his destination; the place where the prophecy had been foretold.

The First Seal

Matthew began a slow death march; his body dragged in hesitation. He did not look forward to this day. The angels stood on either side of him as they began to sing the prophetic hymn; Matthew looked at the steed, its mane flowed like water as he impatiently awaited his rider. Matthew looked to the soft pallet of soil below his feet; remorse and hesitation lingered within his soul. As he mounted his horse with hesitation, the white steed stomped its hoof several times eager to proceed. He held the reigns as it bit into his hand, sweat beading upon his brow and in his grip. The horse shook its head as if impatient; Matthew wished this day had not come, but he knew it was inevitable. The steed sneered as the smoky mist exhaled from his nostrils. God nodded. "It is time, Matthew."

Matthew looked with pleading eyes as if to say, "Not now, not at this moment." But he knew he could not disobey, and without hesitation, he commanded his steed forward. The horse reared in rage as it let out a blood-curdling whine; the front hooves hit the ground like thunder as the horse galloped forward.

Its eyes displayed a dull red glare as the smoke bellowed from its nostrils, with each hoof drop clasps of thunder proceeded. It had begun the first seal had been broken.

Chapter 1: Recruitment

May 2024

Marek sat in a corner booth table, dimly lit, and isolated from the crowd, café located on the Southwest side of Houston, Club Dialo's. It was a nice not-too-upscale place the two would visit from time to time. They had great drink specials, and the DJ played the best in R&B, Hip Hop, mix. Grown folk music, as Marek calls it. Marek sipped on his Hennessey Black and Sprite as Maze featuring Frankie Beverly's "Family" soothed in the background. Marek slowly bobbed his head to the beat of the music. Mummers mingled in the sound of the music as people trying to hold conversations competed with the volume of the music but to no avail. He looked around the club hoping to spot a familiar face from his past or a new face to take home for the night. The women were showcasing. Most dressed to impress while others were broadcasting everything they had by exposing flesh just a thread shy of being butt ass naked. As he was about to look down at his drink, he did spot a familiar face.

"Mallory!" Marek shouted.

The dark-skinned well-built man walked toward his booth; standing six two, he had the aura of the type of person you really didn't want to step to incorrectly.

"Marek, nice to see you again, brother. Thanks for meeting me here."

Marek motioned for Mallory to sit. "You're my brother, why wouldn't I not come to see you. Want a drink?"

Mallory nodded. Marek stopped the waitress walking by as Mallory placed his order.

"Seven and Seven," Mallory requested.

Marek waited until he received Mallory's attention again.

"What's so important you needed to meet today?"

Mallory looked down at the table for a brief moment and looked his brother in the eye with a simmer of anger.

"He's back. Silas, he's back."

Marek looked at him surprised. "What the hell? We sent him. I was there when you..."

"I know, I know," Mallory interrupted. "But it gets worse. There is a politician, Jonathan Lucian, he has been grooming for some time now."

Marek looked perplexed for a moment and then his eyes widened. "So, he..."

"Yes, yes, he is," Mallory interrupted once more.

Marek leaned back frustrated. The waitress came by with Mallory's drink and placed both it and a napkin on the table in front of him. Marek instructed her to put his brother's drink on his tab. They waited until she left before continuing the conversation.

The bouncer sat outside the club smoking his cigar mini. A well-dressed man exited a Lexus Z. His suite obviously tailor made with its dark navy-blue color and black patented leather shoes complemented the attire well. He walked up to the bouncer.

"Is there a cover?" the man asked. He had a very proper British accent.

"Naw, bruh, not till after eight," the bouncer replied.

The man smiled and walked into the club. The bouncer chuckled. "This muthafucker here... Is there a cover, ole chap?" he said mockingly.

The well-dressed man looked about the club; he spotted Marek and Mallory and walked toward their table.

"Europhate, what's your ole ass doing here?" Marek stood and greeted his friend with a hug.

"Young enough to give your ass a thrashing! You look well, Marek."

Marek smiled and returned the compliment as he motioned Europhate to join them.

"I take it Mallory told you the news?" Europhate addressed Marek.

"Yeah, me and him were just talking about it... he stated Silas has been spotted."

"Regrettably so. The time has come, gentlemen, and unfortunately, it is not on our side. Currently the prophecy is unfolding right before us, and it is doing so at an alarming rate."

Marek spoke in his ghetto tone, "Ain't no way to slow that shit down somehow? We ain't even close to ready, and besides, the prophecy is not in place yet, the general has not been found."

"Fortunately for us, he has, however, he does not know it yet. Vincent and I, we meet up with him soon, but..." Europhate paused.

Marek looked at him anxiously awaiting him to finish. "But what?"

Mallory finished the statement for Europhate. "We think Vincent is a traitor. Rumors are Vincent has met with Silas several times. Possible it was Vincent that aided in Silas' escape."

Marek leaned back once more. "Damn!"

Europhate smiled at Marek. "No worries, we travel soon to obtain the scroll. It must be deciphered prior to getting it to Megiddo. I will meet up with Tom and Emily in three days."

Marek still held a face of concern. If Vincent was a concern, it would not be a good idea for him to tag along with Europhate.

"No, I will get the scroll, I would draw the least suspicion, besides, you have to provide safe passage for the general. If this Jonathan character is being groomed, we will need to get our soldier up to speed as well."

"Then it's settled, Marek will get the scroll to Tom; Europhate will meet up with our soldier..."

"And you?" Marek interrupted.

"I have to fly to Megiddo; I have to get with a friend of mine. His expertise will be needed."

Marek ordered Europhate a drink. The waitress arrived shortly with his order.

"Gentlemen, until we meet again, let's drink and enjoy for tomorrow is not promised," Europhate toasted.

Their glasses clinked as they continued to enjoy the remainder of the evening.

The Making of a Soldier

Adrian sat at his desk mulling over the tasks he was deemed to accomplish for the day. His to-do outweighed his allotted workday. Adrian was the security manager for his company's IT department. He loved his job and took his responsibilities very serious. He believed in getting his tasks done and hated to procrastinate. Work now and play longer and harder later was his motto. Adrian was a dashing man, his six-foot two-inch frame towered over most of the people in the office. He was a smooth dark-skinned gentleman with a mild disposition. He could make friends with anyone and make them comfortable in any situation. He sat at his desk pecking away on his keyboard as if under a trance.

Deep in thought about what was completed and mulling over what was needing to be completed. Lost in auto mode, his Outlook meeting reminder displayed its annoying ding.

"Damn, meeting in five minutes."

He wrapped up his email and closed his Excel spreadsheet, prepared his Skype for Business, queued up his PowerPoint presentation, logged in as the presenter of the meeting, and uploaded his presentation. Moments later, multiple chimes flooded his computer speaker, initializing people that were joining the meeting. Adrian took a deep breath, exhaled, and unmuted his mic in Skype.

"Good morning," Adrian began.

He began his presentation as he detailed the agenda for the quarter. Adrian outlined the budget and focus on the mission statement. Before long, it was noon. Adrian had two loves—his wife and food.

The company had Murphy's Deli cater lunch. Adrian wasted no time as he grabbed a turkey and cheese sandwich and snagged his chicken and dumpling soup. He walked into the cafeteria and sat at an empty table. He opened his bag and pulled out his sandwich, tore open his condiments of mayonnaise and mustard, and applied each on one slice of bread. He paired his sandwich back together and opened his container that held his chicken and dumpling meal. He was in the midst of biting his sandwich when someone sat beside him. She was tall with long smooth legs that she elegantly placed under the table. Her hair sat neatly on her shoulder as the dark hue shined in the man-made light that illuminated the room.

Her hands were slender and toned. Eyes were dark brown, almost seductive. Her shape was almost unbelievable. Dressed in a soft blue business skirt, her blouse showed just enough flesh to be business respectable and enticing enough to reel in the imagination.

"I didn't mean to intrude, is it okay to sit here?" she asked.

"No, you're good," Adrian replied happily.

She removed the paper wrapping from her sandwich and cracked the tab on her Diet Coke. As she started to take a bite, she paused and smiled as she lowered her head in embarrassment.

"I guess it would help to introduce myself since I so rudely strong-armed your table." She laughed. Even her laugh sounded sexy and mysterious.

"Janice Pinkerton," she stated as she extended her hand in greeting.

"Adrian Grant. Nice to meet you," Adrian replied. "Which office are you with? I have not noticed you here before."

"I am based in the Vegas office. We have budget conferences here once a year. I hate I have missed a few years."

Adrian bit into his sandwich, intrigued he hurriedly chewed his food and swallowed.

"What prevented you from coming, if you don't mind me asking?"

Janice sipped her soda and dabbed her lip with a napkin.

"No, I don't mind, I travel... a lot! I work with the Legal Finance Team, so I venture to some of our remote locations mainly in Europe."

"Ahhh, that will do it," Adrian exclaimed. "So do you enjoy all of that traveling? I mean you must be homesick after a while; at least I know I would."

Janice agreed. "It has its moments, but all in all, it is not bad. I am more-rounded person, I mean with interaction with other cultures, broadening my knowledge of my job, and the opportunities it has provided."

"Makes sense, me I couldn't do it being separated from my wife and kids... not an option for me. Naw, the only travel I wish to partake in would be here in the good ole US of A."

Janice smiled. "I thought the same thing when I was first confronted with my new responsibilities, but as I traveled and saw all of the opportunities that are out there, my outlook on life was changed."

There was a mild silence.

"So you stated you're married?" Janice asked.

Adrian chewed his food and, after swallowing, answered, "Sorry, yes, twelve years next month."

"That is awesome! In today's society, it is hard to date for a few months let alone staying married... for twelve years? That is truly awesome! Please tell me you have pictures?"

Adrian looked surprised; no one had ever asked to see pictures of his family, but she seemed eager and excited. He reached for his phone and pulled up his pictures.

"This is my wife, Stephanie..."

"She is beautiful!" Janice complimented.

"Thank you, this is my oldest daughter, Samantha; the youngest, Alice..."

"She looks like she is a handful. I am certain she has you wrapped around her finger."

Adrian laughed; she had no idea how true her statement was.

"Yes, she does, but she doesn't know that, and I plan to keep it that way."

Janice laughed at his honesty. The conversation spilled over his lunchtime to the point where one of his guys came to retrieve him from his conversation.

"Oh, wow, I lost track of time, I am chairing the meeting, and well, I was supposed to be there fifteen minutes ago."

"I am so sorry for taking up your time, please let them know it was my fault," Janice replied in a very remorseful tone.

"No, you're good, we were bored to death anyway, so this will kind of shake things up... besides, that's fifteen minutes less we will be in it." Laughing, Adrian gathered his trash and placed it in the trash can.

"Well, it was very nice meeting you, Janice."

"Same here, I will be here for the remainder of the week, so maybe we can lunch again?"

"Now that sounds like a winner," Adrian replied.

He walked back to his office and continued with the already late meeting. Although behind in time, he felt good and was able to meet all his objectives and finish his meeting in a timely manner.

Four o'clock. Time crept in like a professional thief. Adrian packed his laptop, grabbed his keys from his drawer, and exited his office. He walked down the cubicle isles that lined either side of the walkway. The artificial barriers mapped out the straight away leading to the front door. He walked to the parking lot and pulled his keys from his pocket. Depressing the button on his remote, he started the car. As he prepared to enter his vehicle, he heard a familiar voice.

"Don't forget... lunch tomorrow!" Janice shouted.

Adrian smiled. "I'm looking forward to it, have a nice evening."

"You as well and kiss the lovely girls of yours for me." Janice stated waving as she entered the hotel shuttle bus.

Adrian waved back and got into his Chrysler Enclave. He pressed the start button and put the car in reverse. He looked in the rear camera that captured the objects behind him as he cautiously maneuvered his vehicle out of the parking space. Shifting in drive, he exited the parking lot and within minutes traveled from the roadway to the highway. Highway 288 traffic is not the best place to be especially after four o'clock. He used this opportunity to partake in one of his guilty pleasures—audio books. He enjoyed being entrapped in a captivating story. He was able to use this as an escape that only he could appreciate. Engulfed in his book, he was home in no time. He sat in the driveway as he was determined to finish the chapter. Fifteen minutes later, he entered the house; Alice, as if on cue, came rushing toward him. "Daddy! Daddy! Daddy!"

Adrian dropped his bag on the floor and embraced his mini-me with open arms.

"Hey, you, how was school?"

"It was fun, we drew pictures today, and I drew a picture of you and Momma."

Adrian smiled. "Really, and I just know you are going to show me your beautiful picture."

Excited, Alice turned away to retrieve it. "Let me get it."

Adrian stood up and saw his wife standing before him; her small size and medium build frame contoured her clothes perfectly. She wore nicely pressed jeans that traced her legs, stopping just above her ankles. Her black polo like shirt embraced her torso as if it were part of her skin. Her breasts were nicely proportioned and fit her body well. Her hair was dark black with a slight sheen that glimmered as she walked. It sat nicely on her shoulder as her hair slightly hid the arms of her glasses. A small piece of hair just above her brow lay gently on her forehead, refusing to obey the order of the rest of the strands that composed orderly upon her head.

"Hey, baby, how was your day?"

Adrian kissed his loving wife as the annoying chants of "Eeewww, that's nasty" echoed from the two girls.

Adrian and Stephanie laughed. "Those are your children," Stephanie argued.

"Don't I know it?" Adrian agreed.

"See, Daddy?" Alice muscled her way between the two so she could announce all attention upon herself.

Adrian kneeled to try and meet her height.

"That's beautiful, baby, I love the colors you used. You have become a very good artist. I am proud of you."

Alice smiled and skipped back to the room to put her picture away.

"Hey, little girl, how was your day today?" Adrian turned his attention toward Samantha.

She walked over to her dad and kissed her still-kneeling dad on the forehead. "It was good, Daddy; I am trying to write a paper for my social studies class."

"How are your grades, still in the running for honor roll again?"

"Yes, sir, so far I am doing good... I mean well... at least that's what Mrs. Grant said."

Adrian hugged Samantha again. "I am proud of you, little girl. Need help on your paper?"

"No, sir, I am almost done.

Adrian stood and smiled down at Samantha. "Okay, let me let you get back at it."

Samantha grabbed her books and walked back to her room. Adrian had a wonderful life. Everything just felt... right. Later they finished dinner, and Adrian helped to prepare the girls for bed. After Stephanie made sure the girls had bathed, he went to the room and kissed each one good night. Adrian walked downstairs and walked into the master; as he went into the bathroom, he closed the door and activated the shower. The water gushed with force from the showerhead.

He waited for a moment for the temperature to increase and measured it from frequent touch from his hand. After adjusting to the ideal temperature for him, he removed his work clothes and placed them in the clothes hamper. He stepped into the awaiting water and allowed the water to pour along his body like a small waterfall. He stood perfectly still allowing the heat to massage his body.

He felt relaxed as the water washed away all his cares and worries generated throughout the day. After a considerable amount of time, he grabbed his face towel, drenched it from the water, and applied body wash on it.

He washed his body with precision. He was a stickler for cleanliness and loved to smell good at all times.

After he scrubbed his body, he reentered the makeshift waterfall and cleansed the soap from his body. He exited the shower and dried his body from head to toe. He moisturized his skin with the lotion his wife bought for him. She loved the smell and how it mixed with his chemistry, so he made certain to wear it more for her than himself. He slipped on a pair of pajama bottoms and exited the bath. As he walked into the bedroom, he found that Stephanie was already asleep. She was a morning person, meaning she took pleasure showering in the morning. It acted as her wakeup call and rejuvenated her with the energy she needed to make it through her day.

Stephanie was a manager for JP Morgan Bank, finance department. She was a walking milestone, the first black female to be promoted district manager for the southwestern region. She manages several offices in Houston and two in Arizona. Adrian thought about their struggles over the years, some good, some not so good.

But they persevered and helped each other reach their professional goals as well as their relationship goals. They have become closer over the years to the point where they were able to complete each other emotionally, physically, and spiritually. Adrian eased into bed, making every effort not to wake her. He gracefully kissed her forehead, turned over, positioned himself in a comfortable spot, and swiftly drifted off to sleep.

Friday Morning

Adrian's sleep was interrupted by the annoying buzz that blared from his cell phone. He lay there for a moment regretting the sound, but he had a busy day planned and it was Friday, finally. He could hear the shower running. Stephanie had beat him out of bed and was engaging in her morning routine. Adrian walked upstairs to awaken the girls for school. The stairs squeaked as he traced up the stairs. He rounded the top of the stairs toward Samantha's room.

"Sam... Samantha, time to get up."

Samantha moaned as she grudgingly sat on the side of the bed. She wiped her eyes. "Morning, Daddy."

"Morning, baby. Get up and get dressed. You don't want to be late."

Samantha shook her head, stood, and walked toward her closet like a drunken zombie.

"Sam, your momma has your clothes hanging on the door."

Samantha looked and grabbed her nicely pressed clothes as they form around the hanger that supported the material with no effort.

After he was certain Samantha was up, he left his major challenge for last—Alice.

That girl could sleep through a hurricane and not move a muscle. On family trips, he would dread having Alice sleep with them. She was the worst when she slept. She would be all over the bed, one minute it was her foot in your eye, next her head laying on your thigh. As they got older, they were able to place her and Samantha in large twin bed to grant her enough room to sleep. As he entered her room, she was true to form. She laid across her bed one leg hanging out of the bed, the other barely balancing partly in, partly out. That girl sleeps badly.

"Alice... Alice... time to get up. Come on, baby girl, it's time to get up."

Finally, there was movement to his commands as Alice slowly stirred. As she raised her head, she let out two muffled farts—yes, Alice was true to form.

"Morning, Daddy."

"Morning, Alice, Momma has your clothes hanging on the doorknob, let your sister help you get dressed, I don't want to hear you two arguing, okay?"

"Yes, sir."

He knew that was an empty promise; neither Alice nor Samantha are the best people to get along with when they wake up, and putting them together? You may as well be prepared for the drama. Because it is destined to be some with those two.

Later in the morning, everyone scurried to leave the house on time. Stephanie rushed the girls out of the house to the car as Adrian followed right behind. Adrian gave a loving smack as he was greeted once more to echoes of *Eeewww* from the girls.

"See you this evening," Adrian stated.

"Okay, have a nice day, I love you," Stephanie replied.

"Love you too."

The morning seemed to rush by, and before long, it was noon. Adrian was engulfed in some procurement requests he needed to review and approve.

"Hey, so this is your office, sorry to disturb you, did you forget about our lunch date?"

Janice leaned inside his office door.

"No, not at all... was just wrapping up," Adrian lied.

"Sure you were." Janice laughed. "Meet me in the cafeteria?"

Adrian shook his head in agreement. He locked his computer and hurried out of his office into the cafeteria. They literally picked up where they left off from the day before. He enjoyed their lunch date, it was a break from the norm, well his norm anyway. With the exception of yesterday, he normally eats in his office, if he takes the time to eat at all.

Janice looked at her watch. "Let me get a move on, we are closing our meeting early today to allow us time to make it through security for our flight this evening. Maybe when you are in Vegas, you can stop by and I can treat you to lunch."

Adrian smiled but was disappointed they had to cut their lunch short. "That sounds like a plan."

Janice smiled. "Great, here is my card with my office and cell. Feel free to call anytime."

Adrian took the card. "I will, thank you."

Janice shook Adrian's hand and exited the cafeteria. Adrian finished his Coke Zero, which had now become room temperature, and deposited his can into the recycle bin. He walked back to his office and placed Janice's card into his drawer and went back to his previous task of procurement approvals.

Over time, Adrian developed a friendship with Janice. She was able to aid in resolving issues that occurred in the satellite offices. She knew key people there that could get things done. In time, it was obvious that his presence was needed at one of the offices due to management change. Adrian was scheduled to travel to Las Vegas to manage one of the satellite offices near the strip later that year. It was good to keep his promise to his new friend. Adrian called his wife before leaving the office.

"Hello?" Stephanie questioned.

"Hey, baby, I am about to leave for the airport. I will be back next Wednesday."

"Be careful and call me when you get to your hotel," Stephanie stated.

"I will, I love you."

"Love you more."

Adrian hung up the phone. The administrative assistant stopped by his office and knocked on his door. Adrian motioned for her to enter.

"The shuttle is here for you."

Adrian grabbed his bags and followed the admin toward the front of the office. As he walked outside, the driver took his bags and placed them in the shuttle.

Adrian walked to the sliding door as he waited on the driver to open it. He boarded the shuttle and found his seat. The driver boarded the shuttle and drove to the airport. After a long wait, he was checked in and within moments was aboard his plane.

Two hours later, he arrived in Vegas. He went to baggage claim and grabbed his bags. He was planning on calling an Uber but figured he would reach out to Janice. He grabbed his cell and called her cell number.

"Hello? Janice speaking."

"Are you always this formal?"

"Hey, Adrian, nice to hear from you. How is it going?"

"Going great, listen, we just landed and I really didn't want to pay for an Uber..."

"Say no more, give me a few and I will swing by and pick you up. What airlines are you on?" she interrupted.

Adrian gave her his airlines info. There was a brief wait, and before long, Janice pulled up. Her white BMW SUV made a calculated stop as she lowered the passenger window.

"Put your bags in the back."

Adrian followed her instructions as she pushed a button to open the SUV's hatchback. The tailgate slowly rose; he placed his bags in back and scurried back to the passenger side. Janice pushed the button once more and lowered the tailgate.

"Welcome to Vegas. How was the flight?"

"Not bad. They have me staying in Treasure Island."

"Treasure Island, it is. Hey, if you are not busy, maybe we can have a late lunch or drinks later."

Adrian smiled. "That sounds great."

"Fantastic. I will pick you up at your room... say, five o'clock?"

"Five o'clock, it is."

The two engaged in small talk as she drove to the hotel.

Shortly, they arrived. Adrian grabbed his luggage, walked back to the passenger window, and bid his ride goodbye. He walked to the counter and began his check-in. He walked to the room and placed his luggage in the closet. He pulled out his phone and called his wife.

"I made it to the room."

"I'm glad, you going into the office... no, wait, it is four o'clock there. Kinda a waste of time."

"Yeah true, I am going to have dinner and drinks with the coworker here."

"Good, enjoy. Have fun for me... hey, it's Vegas."

Adrian smiled. "Yeah, it is. I love you."

"Love you more."

Five O'clock

Janice was prompt five on the dot. Adrian smiled as he opened the passenger door.

"Hello again, sir."

"Hello, and thanks for the invitation."

"Hey, I have to be a good hostess. I figured we can stop by my place for drinks and order in if that's okay. Traffic on the strip is terrible after five."

"That sounds fine."

The evening went well. Janice ordered Italian; she opened a bottle of red wine. They engaged in conversation hitting on various topics—work, family, future goals. Conversation carried over late into the evening.

Janice looked at the clock on the wall. "Look at the time. I can take you to your room, I know you have a busy day tomorrow."

"Yes, I do."

The wine was taking its toll on Adrian. He was feeling woozy. Janice could tell he was feeling the wine and agreed to have him sleep over. Reluctantly he agreed to her request. She escorted him to her guest bedroom and provided towels for him to bathe with. She agreed to get him to the room early enough for him to change and drive him to the office. Adrian thanked her and followed her directions to the bathroom's location. Adrian, still woozy from the wine, turned on the shower and waited on the water temperature to reach its ideal peak.

He undressed and entered the shower. He closed his eyes and allowed the water to cascade his body. He figured the shower would help him regain his senses from the wine's effects. As he stood with his eyes closed, he felt a hand caress his back. He wanted to resist but he did not have the energy or desire to do so.

Slowly he turned around and embraced in a deep and passionate kiss as the water embraced the two nude forms that slowly became one.

Adrian awoke early that morning. The sun barely peeked into the drapeless window. He looked over as Janice lay sleeping peacefully beside him.

He looked to his right at the clock on the nightstand. Six o'clock. He grabbed his phone and checked for any missed calls. Damn one. He listened to the voice mail that was left.

"Hey, baby, it's me. I figured you may have come in late, so call me in the morning. I love you."

His heart sank. He felt bad of what he did the night prior.

Janice turned to greet a distraught Adrian. She looked at his expression and sympathized with how he felt.

"Please call your wife."

Adrian pressed dial and waited on the phone to pick up. After two short rings, a sweet voice spoke from the other end.

"Hey, baby, how did you sleep?"

"I slept well, how about you?"

"Not well, missed you being here."

Adrian really felt awful. "Well, I will be home soon. Let me get up and get moving, my car will be picking me up in an hour or so. I love you."

"Love you more. Enjoy your day. Bye."

Adrian hung up the phone. Janice sensed his despair and tried to ease his pain.

"Adrian, I am not asking you to leave your wife, nor am I trying to disrupt your household. We can keep this our secret. No one has to know."

Adrian felt lower than low, but their encounter was something he had always wanted sexually. Things he remembered doing was out of his wildest fantasies. She reached for him; his conscience was saying no, but the lust building up inside was saying yes.

Janice and Adrian's affair carried on for months after that. The more he and Janice met, the least guilt resided in him until he had no guilt at all.

Months Later

"Hey, I gotta go." Adrian looked at his watch; it was later than he thought. He had not planned on being gone so late.

"Why? Your flight doesn't leave for a couple of hours, you'll have plenty of time to get to the airport," Janice stated with a devilish grin.

Adrian thought about her statement and laughed; the way she drives, he could leave five minutes till and still make it on time.

"Naw, I have to go. When are you coming back to Houston?" Adrian asked.

"Soon, you know I can't leave my man waiting."

Adrian smiled as he continued to dress. He knew what he was doing was wrong, but he was in love, a forbidden love. How can a man love two women equally? Both seemed to complement each other. Selfish thoughts ran through his mind. *I am not leaving my home and she knows that, and she accepts that. She loves me for me nothing more*, he thought.

"Adrian, what are you thinking about?"

He looked at Janice as if she had read his thoughts. "Nothing, why you ask?"

"Are you afraid I will ask you to leave your home for me?" Janice asked.

That's scary, how did she know what I was thinking? he thought.

"No, why would you ask that question?" Adrian replied.

"I can read you like a book, relax, I would never want you to give up your home. You are mine part time; I can accept that. Besides, with our schedules, we could never make a relationship last," she exclaimed.

He knew she was right and really didn't need to comment on it; he just smiled and continued to dress. He began to fix his tie as she walked over toward him.

She softly grabbed the silk material and skillfully tied the perfect knot as she tidied the tie to business perfection.

"That's the way my man should always look, distinguished."

Adrian pulled her close to him and gave a slow and passionate kiss. "You are spoiling me, you do know this."

"That's my job; supply the things you don't get at home."

Adrian felt his heart sink; that was not the truth he wanted to hear. Janice slipped on a sleek sun dress that draped over her creamy white flesh.

She kissed his dark skin softly and passionately. "Are you sure you have to leave?"

Lust tore at his soul like stubborn wallpaper; peeling at his soul as it fought desperately to exit his flesh.

"No, I have to go, if not, I will never leave."

Janice smiled. "We can't have that, then you will never be able to come out and play."

She walked Adrian out into a hallway that was adorned with various paintings, sculptures, and unique décor.

The semi-whitewashed wall was traced with brass runners and cherry-crowned molding that stretched along the walls like a continuous wooded design that seemed pleasant to the eye. They made their way to the large wooded door that displayed a smoke glass design; its intricate sketching of European design mirrored past reflections of elegance that traced neatly within the crowned arch within a burnt brass design. She grabbed her part-time man one last time and passionately kissed him before opening the door to allow his exit.

"See you soon," she whispered.

"I'm looking forward to it," Adrian replied.

He reluctantly opened the door to his Camry rental as he slung his bag in the back seat and shut the door. He looked back at her briefly as he walked to the driver's side and positioned himself in the driver's seat, pressed the start button, placed the car in drive, and pulled away.

As he drove away, he had to clear his mind of the lust-filled weekend he shared with Janice and refocus his mind into family mode. He knew he was wrong, and he wanted to end the affair but didn't know how. Hell, he couldn't understand how it began. Everything seemed to go so fast. As he pondered over his dilemma, he wondered what was going on at home.

Before long, he had made it to the rental at the airport.

He exited the car and walked inside to turn in the keys.

"Good afternoon, Mr. Grant. I hope your day was enjoyable?" the clerk asked.

"It was good; I am glad to be going home," Adrian replied as he handed the keys over to the clerk.

She typed a few items into the system and scanned the barcode on the keychain.

"Okay, Mr. Grant, you are all set. You can catch the shuttle out front to your gate. Have a safe flight home."

Adrian thanked her and walked out to meet the shuttle.

Janice walked up the stairs slowly as if she was waiting on something. The air in the room felt heavy and overwhelming; a slight stench of sulfur wisped in the air like a subtle mist that was abrasive and uninviting. A shadow rushed along the pale wall; she paused and looked to the floor in submission.

"We are wasting time, have you persuaded him to lead us yet?"

"No, master, but I have a plan in mind. If we take away his family, he will despise God and work for us. I have some people taking care of that as we speak."

"Good. Do not fail me, Janice, you shall hear from my son soon."

With that said, the room cleared, the air in the room became light and clear, but Janice's demeanor was filled with fear and concern.

She could not afford failure. Her life depended on it.

Later That Evening

Bodies lie in the fields as the dead smoldered. The strong stench of flesh burned Adrian's nostrils as he navigated through the forest of carnage. Distressed calls of agonizing moans filtered through the air like an unsettling breeze that seemed to captivate every sense in his battle-worn body.

He could feel the pain of anguish with each casualty he passed as the tears of despair filled his eyes like a flooded river that had overflowed its banks. He felt a hand grab his ankle. Startled, he stopped, and with severe reluctance, he looked toward his human trap.

"Help meeee... pleeeease..." The Unknown Soldier's raspy voice hissed just slightly above a whisper but low enough to amplify his agonizing despair. Adrian leaned down and laid his hand upon the soldier's forehead.

"Go in peace, my brother," Adrian whispered, and with that, the soldier smiled and closed his eyes. Death took hold of his soul. Adrian noticed there was a peace that had fallen upon the soldier's face. A peace he could relate to. As the tears flowed down his blood-soiled cheek, Adrian looked toward heaven and smiled.

He awakened with a jolt. Sweat poured from his body as if he had been in a sauna. He had no idea why he had that dream or what it meant. He sat up in the bed filled with fear and doubt. He continued to question the meaning by process of elimination. He started with the obvious solution; maybe it was something he watched the night before, but he remembered he did not look at TV prior to going to bed. Maybe it was something he ate; but he remembered he had eaten an orange and was too tired to eat dinner. Maybe it was stress from the day. *That's it... stress*, he thought. It was a weird way to acknowledge a stressful day, at least that was what he drilled into his conscience to believe. Adrian got out of bed and went downstairs.

He was parched beyond belief. Bordered near dehydration, he grabbed an old Coca-Cola glass from the cabinet. The famous logo was slightly worn on one side. He sat it on the kitchen island and opened the fridge. He wondered what he would drink as he held the door for what seemed to be forever as he studied and contemplated as if he was cramming for a final exam.

"Can we please decide so you can close the refrigerator door? You do not need to air-condition the house that way; we do have central air, you know."

His wife's voice startled him as it echoed in the solemn room.

"I have no idea what to drink. And what are you doing up?" Adrian mimicked her sarcastically.

"I noticed you were not in the bed," Stephanie replied.

Adrian looked at his wife with admiration. Her small five-foot-five stature silhouetted her gown. Stephanie's sleep mangled hair danced in an unorganized symphony. She walked past Adrian in a provocative manner and grabbed the fruit juice from the fridge. Adrian smiled from her seductive play and filled the glass with ice from the icemaker. She patiently waited until he was done and filled his glass with the juice.

Adrian loved his wife and was truly in love with the two lovely daughters she had given him. He often thought how different his life would have been without them. He could not fathom how he would manage without them.

"What are your plans for the day, Stephanie?"

She looked into her husband's eyes with compassion, a glare that hypnotized the very soul of a man. It was the look of true and undying love for her husband.

"I have to do some shopping today, but after that, I thought I would take the girls to the park later today. Do you think you could get off early today to join us?"

Adrian smiled; he could never say no to her. "I will do my best."

Stephanie smiled and gave him a love peck on his lips. She handed him his glass and went back upstairs. Adrian smiled and drank his beverage. The juice traveled his esophagus like a cool empowered river flooding any dry area in his parched throat with soothing relief. His dream seemed like a distant memory not as important as before. He looked at the neon green display on the microwave clock: five thirty.

He walked with some reluctance into the bedroom as the colors danced in the ambiance of the room. He grabbed the remote to the television and powered it on.

The dull thud made by the sudden rush of electrical current shocked the dark screen to life with images of bright colors. The voice of the reporter from the morning news channel shattered the silence in the room.

He walked to the closet and carefully chose his attire from his wardrobe.

The location he was to go to today would not be forgiving to his docker slacks and crisp button-down shirt. Instead, he grabbed a pair of black Old Glory carpenter jeans and a black pullover he had folded on the closet shelf.

Adrian worked for an oil and gas company in the past that delved in everything from pipelines to pet coke, a black sandy substance used for fuel consumption.

Very precious fuel source, but hell on clothes when caught in the fibers. The normal news reports were read like a rehearsed script—the economy, crime, and tips on surviving the chaos that had ensued over the last couple of years. History was made again as the United States elected its first female president. But the enthusiasm was short lived as her inheritance of the nation's problems soon turned from sympathy to disdain as people began to blame her from the last persons administration. It had always been a blame game throughout America's long history.

Adrian shook his head as the bad news continued to bombard the screen emitting solemn feelings of melancholy throughout the once-vibrant room.

Adrian continued to listen to the news report and the bad news that spewed from the TV was like a poltergeist looming in the room. Before long it was 7 a.m.; Adrian left the house in a rush. Traffic was bad around this time of the morning; even with it being summer and no school, getting to work became a chore daily. He started the engine of his Chrysler Enclave as the electrical devices roared to life and illuminated the console. He viewed the camera to make certain the girls did not leave any toys in the drive as he cautiously pulled out of the drive.

Within minutes, he merged onto the 59 freeway and traveled to his destination downtown.

He could not shake that dream and the meaning behind it. He tried to rationalize any idea possible to explain why he had the dream, but nothing could explain it away. Adrian always considered himself a religious man but could not bring himself to attend church. He felt church in this day and age seemed very hypercritical. They teach from the Bible but do the exact opposite of what they teach. He felt that GOD loved all men, and in turn, if we were made in his image, we should love and respect each other, but unfortunately, we were not doing this. There was more strife in the church in most cases than there was in the world and that was what turned him off from going to church. Pastors who fell from grace being ridiculed by the congregation on the sins the pastor committed; when it was the same people coming to the pastor needing guidance and forgiveness for the sins, they needed prayer for.

Hatred had spread like a cancer among the nations. The United States had simply self-destructed. Caught in the grips of greed and selfishness, they began killing each other off. Adrian was forever the pacifist. He always tried to find the good in everyone. He believed not all people could be as bad and as evil at heart. To his dismay, a civil war had begun to take place.

The dreaded race wars had begun.

The president did what she could to maintain peace and unity, but it was much more than even she could handle. Militant groups started coming out of the wood works, killing any and all minorities they could find.

Black and Hispanic street gangs that were once enemies began to unite turning the streets into rivers of blood.

Although street savvy, they were no match for the well-trained well-organized militant groups.

The New World Order took shape, and all was lost from that point.

Stephanie gathered the kid's things and placed them in a tote bag. She ran over her mental checklist to make certain she had not forgotten anything. *Snacks, change of clothes, toys, keys... keys... where are my keys?* She looked on the dresser and there before her was her keys. She snagged them as if someone was going to take them from her again and headed out of the bedroom. The girls sat at the table as they finished up the bowl of cereal Stephanie had fixed them just moments before.

"Okay, ladies, let's go, we have a busy day today."

"Momma, where are we going?" the eight-year-old Alice asked with excitement.

"You will see," Stephanie replied. "Hopefully, if your dad gets done in time, he will join us."

Alice's face lit up with excitement. Samantha, on the other hand, was engulfed in her bowl of cereal as she snickered at the cartoon that blared from the television. Sam, as they like to call her, was an exceptional child. She loved reading and was very talented when it came to drawing and poetry.

Adrian and Stephanie had a very hard time believing she was just six. Adrian would tease her, stating she had been here before.

"Sam, let's go," Stephanie commanded.

"Yes, Ma 'me," she replied.

They exited the house in a rush as Stephanie aided in getting the girls situated in the car. Stephanie had a million things rushing through her head. She was glad she had taken off for the day. She missed her time with the girls. She opened the driver's side door of her champagne-colored Lexus. Her body meshed into the leather material as it hugged her with security and comfort. She looked at her rear-view mirrors with disgust.

"Why your daddy can't put the mirrors and seat back the way I had it... Ooo, that man!"

Alice and Sam snickered at their mom's comment. They knew that their dad does that on purpose to irritate her. Stephanie pressed the button to raise the garage door. She slowly pulled out of the garage and within minutes was on her way to the park. The girls sat in the back as they entertained themselves with the toys Stephanie had packed earlier.

Stephanie looked in the rearview with love as she viewed the girls. She smiled as she redirected her attention to the road ahead. As she glanced down, she noticed that she was near empty.

Damn it, Adrian! she thought. She noticed there was a gas station ahead. Stephanie put on her right turn signal and merged into the lane, granting her access to the station's entrance.

She pulled to the pump and grabbed her card.

"Mommy will be right back," she stated.

She exited the car and walked to the pump. She inserted her card and followed the ritualistic steps needed to make her purchase. Upon completion, the display illuminated its approval as she grabbed the nozzle, removed her gas cap, and pumped her gas. She was so deep in thought that she did not notice the vehicle that had pulled on the opposite side of the pump. The driver and his occupants exited the vehicle. They were dressed in all black with black steel-toed boots. They were tattered with various Arian tattoos and markings.

"Look here, fellows, a high-class nigga gal. Where you headed, nigga gal?" one of the men sneered.

"None of your fucking business," Stephanie replied. She completed her task and got back in her car, started her vehicle, and drove off. The men looked at each other and got back in their car to give chase to Stephanie.

His wife and kids were on their way home and were caught amidst a group of skin-head radicals. They were recruits trying to make themselves known.

They pulled his wife out of the car and raped her in front of the children. After each one took their turn on his wife, they slit her throat and made the children bathe in her blood. Then in one fell swoop, they decapitated the children and set their bodies on fire.

When Adrian heard of the manner of their death, he became enraged. He wanted revenge plain and simple. He knew the nation had gone to hell in a handbasket and forgiveness was simply out of the question. As each day passed, the hatred in his heart grew stronger. Murder was no longer a taboo in his eyes. Day in and day out Adrian would venture out trying to avenge his pain, his hatred, his loss. Yet he never could muster up enough courage to kill anyone.

He began to lose interest in things he once enjoyed. The hatred seemed to consume every ounce of his being. He viewed people he would meet in a different light. He questioned their true intentions toward him. His happy-go-lucky demeanor seemed to gradually change into a cold and almost heartless emotion. Each time he would close the door to his home, the emotions would rush him like a tidal wave as he would break down and cry each time.

He knew it was not healthy to hold on to so much hate, so much pain, but it was as if he could not shake it—he refused to shake it.

One afternoon he walked in his neighborhood hoping and praying he could meet the men responsible for the death of his family. The only enjoyment he received in life was the walk down the nature trail that led to a wooded area near his home. It reminded him of the walks he shared with his family in the evenings after work.

He cherished his memories now more than ever.

The longing for his family and the deep love he had for his wife seemed to keep him in moments such as these. He wanted relief from the painful lose of his loved ones. Fortunately, this was the only consolation he could get for the moment.

"It must be Christmas!" a voice shouted.

Before Adrian knew it, five men ran from the dark foliage. Anger and hate seethed from their eyes.

"Santa must have heard us. We wanted a nigga for Christmas and look what showed up. We must have been good this year, fellas!"

Adrian's fist clenched as he bit his bottom lip.

"We have a fighter! This nigga is angry! Well, let's calm this nigga boy down, boys."

Before they could proceed, a medium-sized white gentleman came from nowhere and touched one of them on the shoulder and immediately the skinhead fell to the ground dead.

Then almost immediately another black gentleman came and stared at one of the other skinheads. His eyes became bloodshot red soon, the skinhead began to tremble fiercely, and shortly there was a loud pop as he fell to the ground. The other three started to run, but a flash of fire and brimstone fell upon them as their flesh burned to a crisp powder.

Adrian was scared shitless! He fell to the ground, afraid the same fate would happen to him.

"Get up," a voice spoke.

Adrian slowly rose from his cowardly state.

"Your hate would have consumed you and we were not about to let that happen. Your faith has been tested, but you have a long way to go. You must be strong and vigilant. This country is in peril and cannot be saved. You must travel to Europe and prepare for the last battle. You will be informed about the role you will play in this battle. But for now, you must leave."

"Who are you? And how in the hell am I supposed to get to Europe? I can't rub two nickels together to make a dime!"

The black man smiled and extended his hand. "My name is Europhate, and he is Vincent. We are God's angels, sent to watch over you and guide you and to prepare you for the coming days."

With that, he placed his hand on Adrian's chest. The pain was intense, he felt the coldness shoot through his body. It felt as though he was near death, but his inner soul burned like a million flames pulsating fiercely. Adrian's body slumped to the ground. Vincent walked to him and placed in his hand gold coins. "Use these and nothing else. The code is being enforced. You will eat where we instruct you to and sleep where we guide you. Leave here for this country will be no more."

With that said, Europhate and Vincent disappeared. Adrian sat there for a moment. His mind was in a daze. He could not grasp what had happened. He stared at the coins placed in his hand by Vincent.

"Who would take this as currency and why?" Adrian slowly got up from the ground and looked at the remains of the victims lying on the ground and the remnants of what was left of the other three. Why him? Adrian kept asking himself the same question as he walked back to his home.

Filled with more questions, Adrian wasted no time as he went upstairs. He packed a small bag, secured the house, and got in his vehicle. His mind filled with awe from the events that took place just minutes before; he drove to Hobby airport puzzled. Adrian parked his vehicle in the parking lot and took the shuttle to the terminal.

He felt no one would take gold currency. He examined the currency more closely.

They had strange symbols on the face of the coin. Symbols he was not used to seeing before. He knew he had to trust the instructions of the visitors, but he still had severe doubts. His belief was shaky, but he knew he should not disobey what was instructed of him.

"Good evening, may I help you, sir?"

"Yes, I would like a ticket to Amsterdam please."

The clerk typed a few times on her computer. "I have a flight that will be leaving here at 5 p.m. if this is okay."

Adrian looked at his watch. It was 3:45 p.m. "That's fine."

"How would you like to pay, cash or credit?"

Adrian reached in his pocket and pulled one of the gold coins from his pocket.

He handed her the coin. She looked at the coin and, without another word, printed his ticket.

She leaned toward him and in a light whisper, "You will pay with this currency and only this currency. The code is in place."

She leaned back and smiled.

"Will there be anything else, sir?"

Adrian looked at her in bewilderment. "No, that will be all, thank you."

"Heed Europhate's words," she whispered. "Have a nice day, sir."

Adrian smiled and walked away. Still in shock as to how the clerk knew Europhate, Adrian made it to his gate and sat down. He noticed a rather large group of people congregating around the television. Curious as to what the buzz was about, he walked over. He noticed the breaking news banner as it scrolled across the screen.

The president gave her speech. Her face was filled with pain and worry as she spoke into the camera that represented the masses of the fallen country.

"My fellow Americans: It has come to my attention that the inevitable has come to pass. As you are now aware, the universal currency has been accepted throughout the world.

"The countries denouncing the currency, United States, Zimbabwe, Great Britain, and Canada, are slowly being influenced.

"Our very way of life is being torn apart. The constant uprisings of fascist militant groups are taking over the very essence of our country's morals. But I will die to preserve the safety and value of our forefathers. We are not a nation of hate, and it will not be our demise, but through faith, respect, and understanding, we will overcome this obstacle of hate and death and promote love and peace for all mankind..."

Her speech was sincere, but pain and agony mapped her face, each wrinkle told the agony of her countries' centuries of pain and struggles of all races.

"God help her," Adrian thought as he went back to his seat. He knew it was a losing battle. Before long, he heard the announcement for the boarding of his plane.

Adrian looked back only once. He was leaving behind his life, his memories, and his pain. As he boarded the plane, he thought of his wife and kids. How he would miss them. He examined the isle numbers until he found his seat. He feared the unknown; but he knew that fear is what made us human.

He had to keep that in mind. He must never lose his humanity. Before long, the plane taxied down the runway and he was airborne. Europe was a new world for him. He didn't know what to expect, but he knew he would find out soon enough.

The Candidate

The crowd was abuzz as the small middle-aged man walked to the podium. His 5'5" stature demanded little in the way of human presence. He wobbled to the podium in his tan-colored blazer and navy-blue slacks. His receding hairline fought violently to keep his unmanaged swirl of hair in place. He reached into his jacket pocket and grabbed a simple-looking pair of reading glasses. He shuffled his paper and adjusted each page by order he was to read from. He carefully adjusted the microphone and tapped on the head of the mic to get the people's attention. He cleared his throat slightly as he glared over the podium upon the crowd below. The room gradually began to go silent as the back feed from the microphone echoed in the crowd.

"Hello and welcome. God, it's good to be an American! Don't you agree?" he pronounced in a lazy Southern slang.

The crowd erupted in applause.

"Our country has been overrun with false ideas and hope. We miss presidents who represented our beliefs and our values, Ronald Reagan, George H. W. Bush, and George W. Bush. We have lost the White House to inconsistent thinkers who want to turn our country into a cesspool of lazy people who don't respect the true American spirit of hard work, determination, sweat, and grit that made this country great. We were tarnished by Clinton's idealism and Obama's 'Change' and now we have Nancy Grey who believes in a fair playing field for all.

"Welfare is not a fair playing field, people need to get up and work, contribute to our countries economy and not siphon from it. Regulate immigrants from coming into our country... If you can't learn the language, pay our taxes, and contribute to our economy, do not come here."

There was a large roar from the crowd as they applauded the speaker's gesture.

"It is time to take our country back; it is time to take our White House back. Ladies and gentlemen, I would like to introduce the new face of America; a name that will bring back our morals and beliefs, a name that will restore the true meaning of the phrase 'American Can-Do Spirit,' a name that will restore the true meaning of democracy. A name that will restore the faith and freedom in these chaotic times.

A name that will define justice, bring about peace, and allow us to take back these United States. Put your hands together for your candidate and mine, the next president for these God-loving United States of America, join me in welcoming Jonathan L. Ahriman III."

A tall dark-haired man slowly rose from his seat and waved to the crowd. His 6'2" stature and slight athletic build towered with gallantry as he waved to the crowd.

His charming features and strong bone structure commanded respect.

As he walked toward the podium, the crowd went wild with enthusiasm. He continued to wave as he shook the speaker's hand. He graciously thanked the crowd over the applause and waited for the crowd to settle down before he began to speak.

"My fellow Americans: for too long we have watched as this country has fallen into despair. We have lost so much in the way of jobs going overseas, income limited to our American workers, and respect of our country's 'can-do spirit' tarnished and thrown to the wayside. We have suffered too long from the likes of Clinton, Obama, and Grey. It is time we took back what is ours. We need to restore the true meaning of what it is to be an American. We built this country, and I be damned if we lose it in this manner."

The crowd erupted with cheer as he looked upon the people with content. Slowly the crowd silenced to allow him to continue.

"Now I am not trying to promote hate, that is not what this campaign is all about, but I am trying to show to the people of this great nation and to the world that we built this country, through hard work, through perseverance, through dedication. This is the greatest country in the world, and it is time those 48 percent who voted for Grey realizes that she is running this country into the ground. We must pick up where Bush left off, gain the respect this country has been known for, and lead this word we know and love as democracy across every rice patty, every mud-filled river in Africa, every communist country in Asia, and stand on the forefront as the new leader of the free world. Elect me in office and I guarantee to you as Americans, you will prosper, your children will be safe, and you will see the change needed in the White House.

"I thank you, my campaign thanks you, and may God bless these United States of America." His body cringed after saying that last phrase. *God bless America, what a fucking joke!* he thought.

The crowd roared in applause as the man waved to them and smiled. Men from the venue ran to him, eager to shake his hand and congratulate him on a riveting speech.

Jonathan walked off the stage and was escorted to his dressing room. He was seated at the table located in the center of the room. Within minutes, a fairly attractive woman walked into the room.

"Senator, here is your itinerary for the coming days. You have an interview with Rush Limbaugh on Thursday, a political panel with Fox on Sunday, and a few lunch engagements with the NWO next Monday."

Jonathan smiled. "Thank you, Janice. Oh, any word from my father?"

Janice smiled. "Yes, he realizes the time is almost here. Everything is in place. His persuasion of Senator Greenhouse is going as planned. It won't be long now before you are the next president of the United States."

"Good, keep me posted."

Janice smiled and exited the room. Jonathan looked at the gold diamond-encrusted ring on his finger and smiled again. He knew the time was near and he had this country eating right out of his hands.

Friday, February 2028

Jonathan sat in his office feverishly clicking away on his wireless mouse. He would pause for a moment, read, and scribble notes on a notebook. He would stop for a moment grabbing a large bible-shaped book and flip through a few pages. Using his index finger, he traced the pages until he found the information he was looking for. He tapped his finger on the page a few times and leaned back in his chair. Could this be what he was looking for? His thoughts were interrupted by a knock on his office door.

"Yes," Jonathan muttered.

A slim but fit woman opened the door.

"They are here."

Jonathan smiled. "Send them in."

Two gentlemen walked into Jonathan's office. One in a gray business suit tailored to fit with gold cuff links. His shoes wear glistened from the light as the freshly polished finish made him look well kept. His hand was adorned with a single ring gold with a unique emblem design in the center of its facet. The other gentleman was much more casual with slacks, a button-down shirt, and loafer-type shoes. He too also had the same type ring on his right index finger.

"Jonathan." The well-dressed man extended a handshake greeting. Shortly the casual man followed suit.

"So you wanted to meet with us, you say you have a proposition to help propel our cause. I find that will be a challenge seeing as no one knows who you are in the political arena. I mean, how can you help us?"

Jonathan smiled. "Let's just say I have connections, people who can make things... happen. Mr. Greenhouse, I can make you a very powerful man if you can meet my terms, of course."

Mr. Greenhouse sat back in his seat and clasped his hands together and smiled. "With my associate here, I am certain we can make the necessary arrangements; however, we need some guarantees as well."

Jonathan listened intently. "Let's hear it."

The casually dressed man spoke first. "We need some sort of good will gesture that our organization will be able to operate with total and absolute resolve, no government interference or retaliation."

"Done. Next?" Jonathan agreed in a cocky voice.

"I have been eyeing an office seat, upon your election, of course," Mr. Greenhouse slyly suggested.

"Don't worry, gentlemen, I will be elected, and you will get what is coming to you," Jonathan assured.

Mr. Greenhouse and the other gentleman looked at each other with concern from Jonathan's comment.

"Gentlemen, don't concern yourselves, you will receive your requests and much more. Just as long as you take care of my... little problem."

The casually dressed man replied, "Consider it done." He pulled out his cell and pressed a preprogrammed number. "It's a go." And he disconnected the call.

"See you in the White House, gentlemen." Jonathan laughed as he escorted them out of his office.

Once the door closed, Jonathan spoke aloud. "It is time, Father."

"Good, I will join you shortly," a voice replied.

Jonathan smiled went back to his desk and continued on his previous task.

Sunday Evening

Adrian landed nine hours later in Amsterdam. He left the plane and walked aimlessly through the airport. The program on the television caught him in midstep. He sat in awe as the ticker scrolled across the screen.

U.S. President Nancy Grey and Vice President Thomas Greene were assassinated by a fellow politician. Congressman John Grenhouse (R) was detained by secret service officials. No word yet on why he killed the president, but sources state he is affiliated with the New World Order that has taken control of virtually all political standings in this country.

No confirmation has been made of who will take power at this time since John Greenhouse, the Speaker of the House, is a known affiliate of the New World Order. Sources speculate there will be severe turmoil in the House and the Senate if he was sworn in as the president. We will bring more as the story develops.

Adrian felt empty inside. He knew the end was near. He felt that same feeling of remorse for his country. He knew there was no hope, no future. It was just a matter of time. Adrian clenched his bag and proceeded out of the terminal.

He had no idea where he was going or what he would do. He hailed a taxi and asked to be taken to the nearest hotel. Keeping in mind what Europhate told him, he proceeded to give the driver a gold coin. The driver smiled and gave it back to him.

"Time is wasting. You must go. He will tell you where."

Adrian smiled and thanked the driver. Conversation was brief as the driver took him to the hotel. Adrian learned very little from the cabbie. Before long, they pulled into the circular drive of the Amsterdam Suites.

Adrian thanked the cabbie and departed the cab. He walked to the counter in a hesitant manner.

"May I help you, sir?"

Adrian looked toward the floor lost in the events that had taken place since the departure of the airport.

"Yes, I would like a room for a few nights please."

The clerk smiled and began to type. Her fast keystrokes seemed to glide effortlessly across the keys as she pulled up the available rooms.

"May I have your identification please?"

Adrian reached for his wallet and pulled out his driver's license. The clerk looked at the ID and typed again.

"And how many nights will you be staying with us, sir?"

"Seven!" a voice boomed from behind the clerk. "I got this, Sarah, thank you."

A blond-haired man walked toward the counter. He looked like he was in his mid forties. His distinguished attire indicated respect and power. He hit the keys on the terminal with authority as he completed the entry Sarah had previously started.

"My name is James Gresham. We are honored to have you at our establishment. We were foretold of your arrival. You are safe here. So, Mr. Grant, we received your reservations and it is all set. Here is your key. Your party will meet you two days from today. In the meantime, please enjoy our city."

Adrian was lost. He never reserved a room and had no idea as to meeting anyone, let alone being in this place for a week.

"I'm sorry, there must be some mistake."

"No mistake, Adrian. Europhate will be visiting you on Wednesday. Please go to your room, it will become clear to you very soon."

Adrian grabbed his bag and key and headed to his room. He walked to the room door and inserted the key card in the strip on the door. The light turned green; he opened the door and walked in the room. He threw his bag across the room and collapsed across the bed. There were so many questions rolling around in his head and very little answers surfaced as well.

Why him? Why did he have to travel to Europe? What was it he had to do that was so important for him to flee the US? He felt exhausted. His eyes were heavy as if he had been drugged. His thoughts began to mingle with the sounds of the room and the city. Before long, he was asleep.

"You ask why?" Europhate's voice echoed in his dreamy state.

"Your faith in humanity was not faltered, but your faith in God was shaken. Your family will never be lost as long as you carry them in your heart. You have been chosen to fight in God's army. The time is drawing near. It is up to you if you wish to partake in the battle."

Adrian could see Europhate's body take shape. He felt light as a feather; his body was at peace. There was calm in a colorless mist. He felt there was no more pain, no more sorrow.

Just calm he could not explain.

"Adrian, if you are willing, I can show you the powers I have bestowed upon you, but only if you wish to use them."

Adrian could finally make out Europhate's silhouette and began to speak.

"Why have I been chosen? I am far from a saint, I have done my share of dirt in the past, and I have so much anger and hatred in my heart. I am not certain I can guarantee I may not go back and kill those who took from me."

Europhate looked at him and admired him for his honesty. "You won't. I have faith in you, but you must also have faith in yourself. I will give you time to consider; if you accept, you will receive a visit from me in three days."

"And if not?" Adrian asked.

"I have faith in you, Adrian."

And with that, Adrian awakened from his slumber. He sat up in his bed thinking about the dream he had, or what he thought was a dream. He looked at the clock. Ten p.m. He felt rested and at peace with everything.

He felt a calm he could not explain. He went to the bathroom and splashed water on his face. He figured he would go to the lobby and get directions on the nearest restaurant that was open at that hour. Adrian walked to the elevator and pressed the button. As he entered the elevator, he could not get over how at peace he felt. The dream felt so real. He arrived at the lobby and walked to the desk.

"Mr. Grant. Nice to see you, it seemed you hibernated in your room."

Adrian smiled. "I guess I was really tired. Is there a restaurant open at this hour?"

"Yes, sir."

The clerk pulled a map and began to explain to Adrian the restaurants open at the time and how to get to them. He recommended one place in particular that he must try. Trusting the clerk's judgment, he proceeded to the suggested place.

Adrian followed the directions given by the clerk and turned down a rather dark alley.

He figured the clerk wouldn't steer him in an unsafe environment, and if so, he was certain he would have warned him ahead of time. Adrian walked down the dark alley. He could feel a presence that seemed cold and evil. The peace he once felt seemed to fade as he walked further down the dark alley. Voices of ominous laughter echoed from within the shadows. He felt an icy-cold presence he could not explain. Adrian's heart began to beat faster as he tried to continue through the dark tunnel-like walkway. Without warning, a force hit him in the chest propelling him into the brick wall. Adrian hit hard. He took a moment to gain his bearing. As he looked up, he saw a figure walking his way.

"You're weak. You don't stand a chance. How in the hell can you fight for anybody? Look at you. You sorry-ass nigga, you couldn't even protect your own family. How in the hell can you fight for anyone? You niggas are all alike, can't stand for shit. You will destroy your own kind to get ahead. Yeah, you niggas are all the same and you're no different."

Adrian had heard enough, his anger raged in him. Overtaking his fear, his eyes burned his soul felt like fire, but his body felt like ice.

"I'll be damned if I let you take me!" Adrian yelled as he threw his hands out toward the encroaching figure. A bright light lit the alley like the rays of the sun as the ominous figure screamed in sheer agony.

Within moments, the figure disappeared, and the alley grew dark again. Adrian's body temperature regulated. He stood there with a blank look on his face. He was in awe. He had no idea what happened or what he had done, but whatever it was, it worked.

He turned around and went back to the hotel. Adrian rushed inside and nearly encountered the clerk in a collision. The clerk smiled. "Enjoy the shortcut?"

Adrian looked at the clerk. "What the hell just happened?"

The clerk smiled. "No, you mean who in the hell happened? They know and they are after you. You must decide quickly."

"Decide what?!" Adrian screamed.

"Are you joining the final battle? Will you fight?"

"Fight for whom, joining what battle?"

"The battle of Armageddon. You have been chosen among the few to take up the fight against the anti-Christ. This is the beginning of the final days. The prophecies are coming to pass. You have been given a gift that very few possess, and he knows this."

"Who is he?"

"You know of whom I speak! You must decide. Time is of the essence."

"And if I agree to fight? What then?" Adrian asked.

"You will be shown in time," the clerk replied.

Adrian was confident he would join God's army; that wasn't even a factor on that part. His main concern was how he was going to fight and with what. His faith was shaky and hate still filled his heart at times, but he knew he had to control it. He needed that calm again.

"I accept, but what do I do?"

"He will visit you soon. But first, let's get you some food."

The clerk led Adrian to the dining area and sat him down.

He left him for a moment to prepare his meal. Adrian sat with his head in his hands. He slowly looked at his hands and thought back at what happened in the alley. He had no idea what he did or how he did it. Before long, the clerk came back with a nice hot meal. Adrian prayed and then began to eat. The clerk began to explain the things that were taking place at the time. "With the president and vice president dead, the New World Order was put into place. Death was inevitable. Martial law was put into effect as men, women, and children were slaughtered in the streets. Cities burned and states tumbled one after another as the order took reign overall. Those that managed to escape fled to Europe to go into exile. The anti-Christ will soon be put into office. It is the NWO's job to put him into place. In time the radical militant groups will become one with his army and all that oppose him will be executed.

"That is why you must not waste any time. You will meet with Europhate soon. Right now, eat and get plenty of rest. You will need it."

Wednesday, December 2017

Adrian sat in his room looking at the news broadcast as his worst fears had come to pass. It was just as the clerk explained to him.

The NWO had taken control of the government and martial law was passed. Adrian shook his head in disbelief.

There was a knock on the door. Adrian grabbed the remote and turned down the volume.

"Who is it?"

"The one you were expecting."

Adrian smiled. He knew who it was. He opened the door. Standing before him were Vincent and Europhate. Adrian invited them in and closed the door.

He had so many questions to ask but did not know where to begin.

Vincent smiled at Adrian and raised his hand. "Before you begin, let us explain what took place in the alley and how you defeated the demon that tried to attack you."

"That was a demon?"

"Yes. It seems he wanted you as well. Your embedded hatred can be used for good or evil, but it was up to you on how you choose to channel it.

"However, you are not out of the woods yet. You will be tested at every turn. We can't control your actions. God gave man free will, and it is up to you what you choose to do and how you choose to do it."

Adrian sat on the side of the bed and looked toward the floor. He knew his hatred almost betrayed him in that alley. He thought back to his family and the tragedy that came from the same hatred that took them from him.

"How can I know when to fight? I am afraid I will not be able to control my anger."

"You will have to decide. That is the only thing we cannot give you, but what we can supply you with is a means to fight. Europhate has given you the angel's fury. You used this in the alley. This is activated when addressed by a demon, but I caution you, it can also be triggered by hate from humans, so please be careful."

"But how will I know the difference between a demon and human? Don't demons take on human forms at times or even worse possess humans?"

"That's where I come in," Vincent exclaimed. And with that, Vincent touched Adrian's chest. Adrian let out a yell as the pain resonated in his chest. It lasted for a few minutes. Vincent removed his hand. You have been given the Veiled Sight. You will be able to tell a demon if confronted. You will be tempted at every turn, and it is up to you to decide your actions."

Adrian regrouped from the intense pain. "Does it have to hurt so?"

Vincent smiled. "Your body will adjust. For now, sleep. The clerk will tell you where to go from here. Heed my words, Adrian. You will be tested by him and from within. Be very careful who you trust. Not everyone is for your best interest."

"How will I know who to trust?"

Europhate touched his shoulder. "When the time comes, you will know."

With that, they slowly rose and left the room. Adrian was dumbfounded. He knew every action he took would be important. He had to be very careful and discrete. He plopped on the bed looking at the ceiling. The events on the TV echoed throughout the night as he tossed and turned. He had no idea where he was going next, but with his fear, he felt assured he would not be led astray.

The anticipation of what lied ahead made his heart race. Expecting the unexpected, he knew he was still human just from that feeling alone. Humanity will keep him alive. At least he hoped it would.

Chapter 2: The Journey

Chaos had truly ensued. Confusion had taken hold of the human race as disease and famine ran rampant throughout the world. Religious groups tried to unite as one as radical groups chose sides to determine the final battle. Many were confused on whom to follow. Uncertain as to who is right or wrong. Extremist groups that did not follow the code were executed. The anti-Christ had obtained power, and people were swayed by his influence and persuasion. He began his run for office as the world felt he was the answer for all their situations. The NWO had gained momentum as they established dominance through fear. Some religious groups who once feared God were now using God to instill fear into others. The Order used terroristic tactics to bring about social change and hide behind God to make their agenda believable. Catholics, Christians, Muslims, Jehovah's Witness, all these multiple religions are becoming no more as religion is now gone underground. Fear has struck a once free society.

Adrian saw these things unfold before him. He was uncertain as to why so many people do not see the obvious. He turned off the television. Once a form of entertainment, it had now turned into a box of ominous prophecy. He had been traveling for the past month, gaining insight on the prophecies unfolding before him.

He opened his notebook and began to jot down his thoughts.

Day 35

I am caught in the developments of the last days. I can't believe what has transpired in the last month. It seems like a dream. I have tried to—he pauses—think about what I would have done to protect my family in these uncertain times.

I am glad that they are at peace. They are waiting on me. Once my job is complete, I will join them. I miss them so.

Adrian sat on the bed as thoughts of his family played in his head like a movie. He closed his book and placed it on the nightstand. As he looked up at the clock, he remembered he had not eaten. There was a light knock on the door. Adrian rose from the bed and walks to the door.

"Who is it?"

"Marek Townsend."

Not certain who he was or who sent him, Adrian hesitantly opened the door anyway.

"How can I help you?" Adrian asked.

Marek smiled. "No, it is more like how I can help you. May I come in?"

Adrian, still hesitant, allowed Marek to come in.

"I guess you are wondering who I am and how I come to know you, Adrian."

Adrian started to talk, but Marek raised his hand to silence his statement.

"I was sent by Europhate. So I need you to listen to me and heed what I have to say. You will befriend what you hate the most. But keep in mind never believe what you see; trust your heart. It will save you in some very trying situations. Also be very careful who you trust. Not all white people are prejudice, and not all prejudice people are white."

Adrian sat and listened intently. "I will keep that in mind. But who are you?"

"Let's just say I am on the same crusade." Marek reached in his pocket and placed in Adrian's hand a piece of jewelry. "You will be needing this, don't fucking lose this or that's your ass. Damn, you remind me of my brother..." Marek smiled.

Adrian looked at the necklace. Marek smiled again.

"Wear this. It will save your life. When you need me, you can find me with this."

With that, Marek placed his hand on Adrian's shoulder and proceeded to the door.

"Remember, be careful who you trust. Not everyone has your best interest at heart."

"So why should I trust you?" Adrian asked.

"That's a good ass question; you will know in time that I mean you no harm... besides, I can't betray my future general."

"So what do I do in the meantime?" Adrian asked.

"Simple, stay alive, careful who you trust, and most important, don't fuck up!" Marek said sarcastically.

"Yeah, simple." Adrian countered his sarcasm.

With that said, Marek left. Adrian had more questions than answers. He waited for a moment before going to the hotel restaurant to eat. As he sat at the table, he thought about the words of warning he received from that Marek person. *What did he mean not everyone had my best interest at heart? I reminded him of his brother. I have never met that man in my life! And what does he mean I am his future general?*

Hours Later...

Adrian sat in a daze. The restaurant was busy as the murmur of people chatting about the day's events traveled in unison with the clatter of plates and silverware.

"Sir... sir... are you all right? Are you ready to order?"

"Oh, I'm sorry. Can I get a steak medium well and a baked potato?"

The waitress scribbled his order onto a makeshift pad. "Anything else?"

"A glass of tea. Thank you."

The waitress took the menu and went to place the order. Adrian scoped out the partially filled room. There were a handful of people sitting enjoying their meals, some talking over coffee. Adrian felt out of place for some reason.

He could not figure out why. The door opened as three men walked into the restaurant. Adrian knew their kind. He knew it too well. The three men scoped the room and zeroed in on him. Two of which gave an evil smile. Before they could make their way to Adrian, a voice boomed out, "Hey, boy! What are you doing in my establishment! We don't serve your kind here. I suggest you leave if you know what's good for you."

The three men smiled. But before they could do anything, the man shouted, "Relax, boys. I got this one."

They smiled and nodded as they took a seat at the bar.

"Come on, boy!" the man shouted.

Adrian's blood began to boil as the man escorted him out to the back of the restaurant.

"Relax, Adrian. I am not trying to become your next casualty. It is not time and you do not need to waste your time with those three. Go to this address, I will join you soon."

"Who the hell are you?"

"Let's just say I am a friend. Now hurry. Go!"

Adrian made haste to the address that was given to him. He knocked on the door. There was a short pause.

"Who is it?"

"Adrian Grant. I was told to come here."

The door opened and a middle-aged lady stood before him. The years of worry streaked her face like tattered words on an aged piece of newspaper.

"Come in, we have been expecting you. You must be famished. Come and sit."

Adrian hesitantly walked into the room. The lady escorted him in and motioned him to sit at the table. Adrian did as she asked.

"Trust me; no harm will come to you. Marek told us to look after you. We were instructed to get you to your next location safely."

"Who are you?"

"Sorry, I am Emily. And the man you met at the restaurant was my husband, Tom. He can be rather... brash, but his heart is in the right place, trust me."

Adrian and Emily talked as she prepared dinner for him. The more they talked, the more things began to fall into place. He learned that they were underground trying to aid future soldiers in the last battle. Marek was the first one they aided. He had been designated as one of the four horsemen of the apocalypse. His family had held this title for centuries. He too tried to deny his destiny that was why he probably took to Adrian. Adrian found Marek was crucial to the development of the prophecy.

"So this is like a safe haven for soldiers."

Emily smiled. "Yes, this is our version of the underground railroad. Only this is not to lead you to freedom. This is to lead you to fulfill the prophecy. You will be tempted, but please believe me when I say you must resist. Our lives depend on it. Europhate and Marek have faith in you. So you must resist; not only for our sakes, but for their sake as well."

"I noticed you did not mention Vincent. Does he not have faith in me as well?"

Emily stopped what she was doing. "We do not mention his name in this house. I suggest you take heed to Mallory's warning. Not all have your best interest at heart. Vincent is..."

"Emily!" Tom's voice boomed.

"Tom... I'm sorry."

Tom looked at her with a stern sense of disapproval. "You have said too much. He must find out for himself. Sorry for the rude introduction, but it was not time to engage in any battles at this time. You cannot be exposed yet. You are not strong enough. I am certain my wife has pretty much told you everything under the sun. She can be a bit too talkative, but she means well. Your belongings will be brought by my daughter. You will lay low here for a few days and then we must get you to Germany. But for now, eat. We will talk more when you are done."

Chapter 3: The Escort–Trust No One

Tom spoke of what Adrian should be aware of on his journeys. He was very vague on his answers to Adrian's questions. It was as if he was trying not to indulge in giving too much information to Adrian.

"Tom, can I ask you a question? Why is it everyone I speak to are vague and evasive?"

Tom looked to the floor as he pulled out his pipe. He tapped it in his hand three times, reached into his pocket, and pulled out his tobacco. He stuffed it in the pipe and struck a match as he took two strong pulls to ensure the tobacco took to the flame.

"Adrian, we try to be evasive to keep from influencing your decisions. Your work is of great consequence and the decisions you make must be made by you, not by our opinions. We can only tell you through instructions given to us—prophecies that have been told that must come to pass."

Adrian rubbed his head in exhaustion.

He knew what Tom spoke was true, but he still did not feel satisfied with his answer.

"Enough for tonight. You must get some sleep. You have a long journey ahead of you."

Adrian looked confused. "Journey?"

Tom smiled. "You thought you would be here forever?"

Adrian had to laugh.

Tom smiled. "My daughter will accompany you. She holds with her the scrolls of Megiddo. Take these to Germany. There you will meet Mallory. He will take it from there."

"Why didn't Marek take the scrolls with him while he was here?"

"He could not risk the thought of being caught with them—especially knowing that the NWO knows who he is."

Tom went over the travel instructions and contacts they would encounter on their trip. Adrian listened intently to the instructions Tom gave to him. Tom was a brash man who did not mince words. However, he was a kind man who cared for the safety of Adrian.

"Adrian, I ask of you one thing."

Adrian looked into the sincerity that displayed from Tom's eyes.

"Anything, Tom. What is it?"

"Please take care of my daughter. Promise no harm will come to her."

Adrian shook Tom's hand. "I promise on my life that no harm will come to her."

Shortly, Tom's daughter came through the door. She looked frail in stature. He realized she was the waitress from the restaurant. Her skeleton frame barely filled her food-stained dress. Her hair was straggly and a bit out of sorts.

But he could tell by her scrappy tone that she was very capable of holding her own.

"Hello, Adrian. I'm Amelia. Seems we will be traveling companions. I suggest you get some rest, we have an early start in the morning."

She kissed her father and mother as she walked past Adrian. "I have secured our transportation for the morning, Father."

"Good. Make certain the scrolls do not leave your side and make certain to look after our soldier. Amelia, promise me you will be careful."

"I will, Father."

Adrian followed Tom to the guest bedroom as he was given his items for use for the night.

"You will leave at dawn. Rest well."

Adrian thanked Tom and prepared for bed. He knew he had a major task ahead of him, and he was eager to get underway. He thought of his promise to Tom. He knew he had to keep it, for Tom's sake. The more he thought about Tom and his family, the more it made him think about his own family. A smile crept onto his face as he slipped into his needed slumber.

Early Morning...

It felt as though Adrian had just lain down when Tom woke him up. "Adrian, it's time. The car is waiting."

Adrian groggy and lacking energy sat on the side of the bed. He felt drained but remembered the promise he made to Tom.

He forced himself to get motivated. He grabbed his bag and headed to the room where Amelia and Tom were waiting. Emily came in later with a small bundle of food.

"Here, this will come in handy on your trip. You two be safe and contact us when you make it."

Amelia agreed and kissed her mother and father. She looked at Adrian with a nod and walked out the door. Tom grabbed Adrian's arm. "Remember your promise."

Adrian reassured Tom his daughter was safe with him. Adrian got in the back-passenger side of the car. Tom hit the hood of the car to signal the driver to leave. The car pulled off. Amelia looked back one last time as the car left the drive. Not much was said in the car between the three.

Adrian was still focusing on the promise he had made to Tom. They arrived at the airport a half hour later. They went through security but were stopped.

"Miss, can you step out of the line please?"

Adrian became suspicious as Amelia did as she was ordered. Adrian knew she had the scrolls on her and was afraid they would confiscate them. He was at a lose. He needed to do something, but what? He grabbed the necklace given to him by Mallory. Without warning, the alarms screamed throughout the airport.

SECURITY BREACH AT GATE 12, SECURITY BREACH AT GATE 12.

Security personnel scrambled to the gate. The security that pulled Amelia to the side left her as they scrambled to the call at gate 12.

Adrian grabbed Amelia by the hand and escorted her through gate 7. They made it to the gate ready to board.

"I am sorry, we are prevented from boarding at this time due to the breach. Please be seated."

Adrian and Amelia sat down waiting to board.

"That was close," Amelia stated.

"Yeah, too close. But we are not out of the woods yet. We have to lay low until we board. We have got to get aboard that plane."

Adrian knew they were fine as long as security was on the breach call, but sooner or later, they were certain to come looking for them. Adrian was trying to figure out a way to keep this from happening. He looked around and saw a familiar face. Marek looked in his direction from across the room and smiled. He motioned toward the counter. There was another steward standing there. Adrian nudged Amelia on the arm and made their way to the counter.

"Adrian, Amelia, this way, please."

The stewardess looked around and hurried the two through a door. She escorted them onto the plane and to the back.

"Wait here, you will be safe."

The stewardess went to the front of the plane and spoke to the pilot. The pilot walked to the back of the plane where the two sat.

"You will be fine as soon as the warning is lifted, we will board and get you guys to Germany."

Adrian thanked the pilot. He knew the real hero was Mallory. Amelia and Adrian talked about the plans to complete the journey to Germany. He learned a lot about Amelia. She was nineteen and was given the scrolls when she was young. She understood the writings and knew she was to transfer the scrolls during the fall of the eagle. Adrian learned the eagle was the fall of the United States.

The Rider of Death was to use the scroll to open the seal. Adrian's job was to protect Amelia to make certain she arrived safely to Germany to deliver the scrolls.

"Why couldn't Marek take the scroll himself? He was already there, it only made sense."

"The NWO knows who Marek is and his objective for the scrolls. He could not afford to be with the scrolls. That would be too great a risk; besides the prophecy foretold of your protection of my journey."

Amelia opened the scrolls and read to him the prophecy. "The soldier will guide the deliverer to the land of chaos. The scrolls will be bestowed upon Death as the prophecy will be unveiled. Megiddo will prepare the armies of the alliance. On the day of the blood moon, the armies will gather in Megiddo. Death will announce his arrival as the battle of battles will soon begin upon the last eclipse of the blood moon."

Adrian sank back into his seat. It was finally hitting him that this was real. Time was really of the essence. He tried to put up a brave front by reassuring Amelia that all would be well. He held her hand as he instructed her to rest.

Adrian closed his eyes as well but knew sleep would not come easy as the prophecy echoed in his mind. Adrian was awakened by the stewardess who had helped them on the plane.

"We will be arriving in Germany shortly, would you care for a beverage or something to eat?"

Adrian smiled and asked for a Hennessey and Coke; Amelia asked for bottled water and a chicken dinner listed on the flight's menu.

The stewardess went into her cart and gave the assigned orders. Adrian sipped on his drink. He knew he really didn't need it, but with all of the spirits he had ran across recently, at least this one will help him relax. Adrian stared out the window his mind seemed to roam.

"What are you thinking about?" Amelia asked.

"Nothing; I am just eager to get these scrolls to their destination," Adrian replied.

He thought about the promise made to Tom. The more he thought about it, the more he thought about his family. How would he be able to protect his family in that situation?

Would he submit his child to voyage on a prophecy that could eventually cost them their lives? He could not imagine anything happening to his own children. Although he felt guilty that he was not there to protect them from their fate. He felt helpless.

He refused to have this happen to someone else's child. He had a choice. He could protect this one and he had the means to do it. He had suppressed his guilt for the loss of his family, made every attempt not to find guilt in himself. He felt he let them down. He knew he could not have saved his family and was certain he would have experienced the same fate they received.

How can man express so much hate to another? Man has so much to atone for no matter the race, gender, creed, or color. We all have much to atone for. No one person is less innocent than the other. He has tried to come to terms with his emotions; no one race should have hatred towards another because of what a small group of idiots believed to be right.

He remembered the phrase spoken by Tom—not all white people are prejudice, and not all prejudice people are white. This has not been a truer phrase spoken as he looked back on all of the help he had received on this journey. He could not help but smile. He was finally coming to terms with his emotions.

He was letting go of his pain, his guilt, his hatred. He could finally let it go.

They arrive in Germany three hours later. The stewardess that helped them in Amsterdam escorted them off the plane. She hugged them both and wished them luck as they made their way to baggage claim. Adrian felt the feeling of peace he had experienced from the dream he had a month or so back. He knew time was of the essence and he finally had some control over his emotions. He knew what he had to do. Adrian and Amelia collected their bags and hailed a cab to venture to their next destination.

"Taxi!" Amelia yelled.

Adrian felt uncomfortable about this taxi. He could not understand why, but he really felt uneasy.

"Not this one," Adrian instructed Amelia. She looked at him with a puzzled look.

"Trust me, this is not the one." Adrian grabbed her arm.

The cab driver sensed who they were. "Stop, thief! Police! Stop them, thief!"

Adrian grabbed Amelia by the arm and began to sprint away from the cab. The commotion drew attention to the airport police. They soon gave chase to Amelia and Adrian. They ducked into an alley between the terminals. A door was open leading to an empty hanger; Adrian knew they were going to be caught.

"Adrian here! Hurry!" Vincent shouted.

Adrian ran toward Vincent, but Amelia snatched her arm out of Adrian's grasp.

"What's the matter, Amelia? What are you doing, let's go!"

"Not with him! No!"

Adrian remembered the words of Amelia's mom, and with that, he stepped back from Vincent.

"Adrian, what's wrong, let's go, they will be here soon."

Adrian looked at Vincent. "How did you know we were going to be here?"

"Never mind all that, Adrian, let's go."

"No, how did you know we were going to be here?"

"Adrian, you've picked a bad time to start taking what I said to heart now. Now let's go!"

Adrian began to back away from Vincent even further. "No. How do I know you are who you say you are? And why is it she does not trust you?"'

"Because the little bitch knows that if she does, she will die. Now give me the scrolls before I kill the both of you!"

"I can't let you do that, Vincent. I will not let you do that. Run, Amelia!"

Amelia ran to the other end of the hangar as Vincent reached out after her. Adrian raised his hand and screamed as an intense beam of light dispersed from his hands, throwing Vincent across the other end of the room.

"Enough, Vincent!" Europhate shouted. "Go, Adrian, get her to safety."

Vincent got to his feet and faced Europhate. "You don't get it, do you, Euro... he prefers them to us. I can't let them take our place! What does he see in them? We were there from the beginning! They don't deserve his mercy, his grace. They need to die!"

Europhate looked at Vincent with disgust. "How could you, Vincent? How could you let jealousy destroy your bond with him? You are just like Lucifer. His jealousy had him lose favor. He never turned on us, Vincent. Never."

Vincent laughed aloud. "Foolish. You're just like them. Don't you know he does not care about us? It has been about them all this time. I refuse to play seconds to any fleshlings!"

Vincent raised his hands, and before he could perform his deed, Europhate's eyes turned red, and Vincent screamed out of pain. By this time, Marek ran into the hangar.

Seeing his friends in danger, Marek summoned Mallory to aid him.

Mallory appeared and not a moment too soon. "Send him, Mallory! Send him now!" Europhate screamed.

Mallory began to chant. The air got dark and heavy as spirits whirled around Vincent. Vincent let out a bloodcurdling scream as they took his body away. Mallory collapsed on the floor exhausted from his summons. Europhate walked over to him to make certain he was all right.

"Good job, Mallory, good job," Europhate stated.

Adrian and Amelia walked over to Marek. "Are you okay?" they asked.

Mallory smiled. "Yeah, it always tends to drain me when I'm called upon. I think you have something that belongs to Marek?"

Amelia smiled and handed the scroll over to Marek. Marek smiled. "You did well, Amelia. But remember your work here is not done, so stay ready at all times. As for you, Adrian, you're learning. Good job."

Adrian smiled from the compliment.

"Don't let that go to your head though." Marek grunted.

Adrian was proud of Amelia and felt a bond he could not explain. She reminded him so much of his daughters. He could not fathom anything happening to her.

Adrian smiled. "Lucky for us Europhate stepped in when he did. I don't think I could have taken on Vincent myself."

"Actually, you could have," Europhate interceded. "You are stronger than you think, Adrian. But enough talk. Get Amelia to Berlin. Amelia, you remember who you are to meet?"

Amelia nodded yes.

"Good. Marek, they need transportation, can you help them in that department?"

Marek threw a set of keys to Adrian. "Be careful with my brother's baby, I only had it a week now and I would hate to hear his mouth if something was to happen to it."

Adrian smiled and thanked them as they went to the back of the hangar and exited out of the back door. Adrian saw Mallory's car BMW 7 series. He and Amelia got in and headed to the highway. Both were glad to be alive, but neither had no idea what to expect next.

Chapter 4: The Meeting

It was a long drive to Berlin. Adrian could not get out of his head what had happened. He didn't know who to trust anymore. He knew his journey was still a test preparing him for the final battle. He didn't know how to look at his new responsibilities. Are they a gift or a curse? He had many questions he wanted answers to, and what was his true role in this final battle?

Adrian and Amelia arrived in Berlin three hours later. Amelia used the GPS to find the checkpoint they were to meet at. An hour later, they pulled up to a small cottage. The grass-hutched roof emanated a dark green color from the hundreds of blades of grass lining up in unison. Amelia smiled as she looked at Adrian. She opened the car door and walked to the cottage door. She knocked three times and then opened the door. No one was inside. She walked in and checked the rooms before lighting a fire in the fireplace. She grabbed a pot and filled it with water. She then went to the cupboard, grabbed a few vegetables, and began to cut them into the pot. She left the cottage for a moment and returned with a piece of cured pork that she placed in the pot. She then took the pot and placed it on a hook inside the fireplace and covered it with a lid. She went back to the sink and washed her hands.

Adrian sat at the table contemplating on what to do next.

"You look worried," Amelia stated, breaking the silence.

"I am. I almost got us killed back there."

"No, you didn't. You didn't know about Vincent."

"Yeah, but I should have. Your parents warned me about him."

"But we didn't die and that's a good thing, right?"

Adrian smiled. "I guess you're right. So whose place is this?"

"This is a safe house. Just like us, the people who live here know of the prophecy. We help believers to get from place to place whenever trouble brews."

Adrian stood up and walked to the corner of the table. "Somewhat like an underground railroad."

"Precisely," Amelia agreed.

"So what is this prophecy? Why is it so important?"

"It is said that the general of God's army will be transported to the battlegrounds to partake in the last battle. He will lead side by side with the four horsemen. Adrian, you are the general. It is up to us to keep you alive."

Adrian felt overwhelmed. He could not understand why he was chosen. He walked out the door and strolled in the backyard. Standing outside was Marek and another man who looked as if he could be his brother. "Adrian, this is Mallory, my brother, he won't be here very long but wanted to meet the prophecy for himself," Marek commented.

"Prophecy? Bloody hell! What's with this biblical mumbo-jumbo, eh, governor? If you ask me—," Mallory ranted.

"But we didn't, so shut the hell up!" Marek interrupted. Adrian, half amused by the two, continued to walk in the semi-wooded field in the back of the cottage. Cloud of doubt resonated in his mind.

"I am no one special. Why was I chosen? Who am I to do such an important task?"

A voice whispered through the slight breeze. "Why wouldn't you be, Adrian?"

Adrian saw an image of an old man walking toward him. He looked worn but really good for his age.

"Who are you, and how is it you know *my* name?" Adrian demanded.

"Why wouldn't he know your name?" Marek stated in a sarcastic manner.

Adrian turned around to Marek. "What do you mean? Why would he know me?"

"You're back," Mallory commented as he walked toward the old man.

"You know him, Mallory?" Adrian asked.

"Yes. I believe you know him too," Mallory answered sarcastically.

Adrian, looking puzzled, asked the old man his name again.

"I am Alpha and Omega, the beginning and the end... ," God answered in a commanding voice.

"Bloody hell! Here we go," Mallory interrupted. "The Great I AM! HE is God, Adrian."

Adrian looked at Mallory as if to say that was rude.

"Don't mind him, Adrian," God answered and looked at Mallory. "We have had our conversation, now it is your turn. You ask why you were picked.

"You were chosen because of your faith. Although you faltered on occasions, you still tried to hold the same belief in humanity as you do now. Faced with adversity and prejudice, you still tried to find the good in humanity."

Adrian smiled at the confidence God had in him.

"I believe the biggest character trait Satan ever bestowed to humanity is HATE. Humanities Answer to Ego and I know having an ego is to Edge God Out, so H.A.T.E. to me is Humanities Answer to Edging God Out," Adrian replied.

"You humans and your acronyms. Clever. Very clever. How do you feel about him now, Marek?"

Marek smiled and shook his head. "I believe he would be a worthy soldier in this battle. Good pick, old man. But you knew that already, didn't you!" Marek stated with sarcasm.

"Well, if you don't mind, I will take my leave. Good luck, 'chosen one,'" Mallory snapped.

God smiled. "Well, I leave you two to discuss your next move. Oh, and, Adrian, there's someone here to speak with you."

A soft and gentle voice whispered in his ear. "Hello, Adrian."

It was his wife. He felt the emotions rushing back into his body the pain, the love, the yearning. "Please don't weep for me, we are fine, and we will meet again soon. We love you, Adrian, and will always be with you. Always."

The tears streaked down his face as he felt the soft touch of his wife's hand on his chest and a subtle kiss embracing his lip. He knew he had to fight.

He knew he had to win.

Marek smiled and walked away to allow Adrian to gather his composure. They had a lot to discuss, and time was of the essence.

Adrian stayed in the garden for hours. He contemplated on the importance of his role. After what seemed to be forever, Adrian entered the small cottage. He looked at Marek with an unexplainable calm over his face.

"I'm ready," Adrian stated with a smile. A feeling of relief graced his face.

Marek smiled. "Eat. We have a lot of training to do."

After the meal, Adrian and Marek trained with the various powers bestowed upon him by Vincent and Europhate. Marek taught him how to conserve his strength after each use. Adrian was not used to the strain each gift took on his body, but he quickly adapted and began to channel his energy with caution, conserving his energy after each use.

Weeks passed by before Marek felt he was ready to continue his journey. Adrian awoke one morning to find Marek gone. He looked around the cottage as he saw Amelia asleep. He ventured into the garden and stood in the spot where he felt the soft touch of his wife just weeks earlier. He touched his hand to his heart and smiled. He stood for a moment and walked back inside. Amelia was up and fixing breakfast.

"Hey, how did you sleep?" Adrian asked.

"Fine. And you?" Amelia responded.

"Good, I guess. Where is Mallory?"

Amelia smiled. "He does tend to grow on you, doesn't he? He has gone ahead. He has his own prophecy to fulfill. Care for some breakfast?"

Adrian nodded his head yes and sat at the table. He knew he had learned all he could from Marek and knew the rest was up to him. Adrian finished breakfast and went into the room to pack his things. There was a knock on the door as Adrian packed the last of his belongings into his duffle bag.

"Adrian, someone is here to see you," Amelia whispered.

Adrian walked into the breakfast area and seated at the table was Europhate. He looked weary and worn. He looked at Adrian with concern.

"Your journey is about to begin. You will be challenged even more than before. I have faith in you, Adrian, but beware, his minions are many and they are very cunning. Take heed and decide with your heart over the obvious. Remember my words for it will save your life."

Adrian took heed to Europhate's warning. Europhate then stood and placed his hand onto his heart. Adrian took the intense pain; his body began to convulse for a few seconds.

"I have bestowed upon you Judgments' Reign. This will prove most useful in your upcoming battle. Take care of Amelia for her task is not yet complete. You will reach Copenhagen for your next task, this is where you and Amelia will part ways. Amelia, you know your task... the prophecy must be fulfilled."

Amelia nodded and exited the room. Adrian was shrouded in a cloud of mystery but knew they would only tell him what he needed to know and no more. Europhate smiled and walked away. Amelia appeared shortly after and motioned to leave. Adrian loaded the car and the two were on their way.

They drove in near silence. Adrian's mind on Europhate's warning. What was to become of Amelia, and what was in store for him after she leaves? There were more questions than answers. He wanted so desperately to ask Amelia what was in store—what the prophecy had prepared for him and Amelia. But he knew she would not reveal that information. They made their way to a checkpoint. Adrian had a very uneasy feeling.

He pulled the car off to the side of the road. Amelia looked at him puzzled.

"Something is not right. Wait here," Adrian answered her concerned look.

He exited the car and walked toward the checkpoint. The two guards had a cold aura about them, an air of death.

"Hello. May I see your papers?"

Adrian reached into his pocket and pulled out his passport. He presented the paperwork to the guard. The guard viewed the credentials and smiled. He murmured something to the other guard in a language that was far from human. Adrian knew exactly who they were.

"Too bad your journey has come to an end, warrior!" one of the guards shouted.

Adrian was thrusted backward as a strong force repelled him to the ground. He knew he had to fight to live. Adrian's body trembled as the sky grew dark; without warning, brimstone showered the two guards, killing one of them and severely injuring the other.

"You picked the wrong person to fight with." Adrian smiled as he approached the remaining demon.

"Have mercy please. I don't want to die. Please have mercy," the demon cried.

Europhate's words echoed in his head.

"Consider this your lucky day. Tell your master I am coming for him," Adrian bellowed.

The demon slowly made his way up and retreated into the nearby brush. Adrian's adrenaline rush began to dwindle fast. His body felt as though he was drained. Luckily the demon had left and did not see him in his current state. He could have easily been defeated. He staggered to the ground. He thought to himself, *Marek would have been pissed at me. I did not pace myself in this battle. I could have been killed.*

Amelia pulled alongside him. "Adrian!" She helped him into the car and reclined the seat back. She positioned him in and closed the door. She looked around to make certain they were not followed. She put the car in drive. They drove without incident to Copenhagen. She drove to the safe house they were instructed to get to. She blew the horn and a middle-aged man emerged from the house. Amelia ran to the other side of the car.

"He fought two demons! But he is weak," Amelia stated.

"Marek and Europhate were right. He is the prophecy. Come let's get him in," the man stated.

The two helped Adrian inside. They guided him to the bed and laid him down. Adrian felt he was in a dream state. He felt like he was drugged, nothing was coherent.

"You've done well, Adrian. Rest." The man's voice seemed to fade in the distance.

Chapter 5: Preparation

The sun beamed upon his smooth brown skin. Cotton and tobacco were the staple crop at the plantation. He kept his head low as he pulled the cotton from the stem. The work was hard and long, but he had a plan to escape. He and his family would be free within a few weeks. His calculation cemented in his head worked as his motivation. Sunset came with resistance as it slowly hung upon the horizon. The slaves in the field gathered the last of the day's product and stored them accordingly. As nighttime blanketed the earth, he waited until he saw the lantern lights were extinguished in the big house. He got his wife and children together, and silently gathered outside the makeshift shed they called home. Several other slaves met up shortly after.

They were to meet up with Moses in the swamps just north of the swamps. They gathered enough food to last for several days and used the cover of night to escape the plantation. The humidity of the night hung around their necks like the chains used to bring them to the plantation. They trudged through the swamp guided by the North Star and audible signals that was used to verify their location. Bird and small animal calls echoed through the swamp carried through the air intermittently as the slaves responded back in turn. Soon they had reached Moses. Harriet Tubman smiled when she saw her cargo.

"We will rest where I tell you and travel when I tell you. Follow my instructions without question and I will get you to freedom," she whispered.

They began their journey through the swamp and traveled shortly along the road using the trees and brush as cover. They made their way to the first safe house. Harriet motioned for them to stay put. She lit her lantern and swayed it from side to side. Within minutes, the lantern was lit and placed in the window.

"It's safe, let's go."

She motioned for the slaves to follow her to the eastern portion of the house where they met the farm owner. He was a tall white man with a gentle disposition. He opened the storage doors that led under the house. The slaves filed in quickly and quietly. Harriet was the last to enter. The farm owner looked around to verify the coast was clear and went inside the house. His wife wrapped salt pork, bread, and water in a small basket and lowered in a hidden hole. Harriet took the basket and divvied up the food among the slaves.

"The women and children will stay here for a day or two. The rest of you will continue with me to the next station. For now, eat and rest, we will travel by night fall."

The farm owner came in with a leather saddle bag.

"I have traveling papers, for the women and children. The other papers will not pass for the men. We can escort them out in two days' time. It is easier to transport the women and children across without raising too much suspicion."

Titus agreed that would be best; it was easier to escort three or four than trying to manage six or eight.

Soon he and his family would be free. Titus embraced his wife and children and drifted off to sleep.

Awakened from what seemed to be a long slumber, Adrian felt rested; almost renewed in a sense. He looked around the room to see if there was any familiarity to his location; there was nothing. He got out of bed and ventured into the next room. He could see various photos that seemed to tell a story of someone's intriguing past. His eyes were fixed on one photo in particular. The date on the bottom right was labeled September 1823. A group of slaves posed at a house. In the middle of the group stood a young man who appeared to be in his twenties standing with them.

"Ahh, you admire my picture. I led many a slave to freedom. It was long and hard work, but if I had to do it all over again, I would. Nice to see you're awake. That battle took a lot out of you, son. You have been sleeping for a few days now," a voice stated to him from behind.

Adrian turned to greet a middle-aged man; he looked to be in his early to mid fifties. He dressed with distinction, at least for that region anyway. He donned a pleaded jacket with a pair of matching pants; the pipe he held in his mouth seemed to be fixed to his lip. He was slightly balding, his facial hair was neatly trimmed and very much with the times as it tapered into a chinstrap cut. Adrian could tell he was desperately trying to hold on to his youth.

"I find it terribly hard to believe," Adrian contested, "that you are in this picture. The date here is 1823 and you are telling me that you took this picture? This has got to be some trick photography."

"It is true, Adrian. It is him in the picture," Europhate boomed as he came into the room. "Say hello to Titus. This is your guardian. You have a lot to learn from him as he will teach you to use your gifts wisely. I was afraid you would not pass your first test, but you did well, Adrian. I am proud of you."

Adrian looked in dismay. How can this middle-aged man standing before him be the same man that appeared in this picture taken almost two hundred years ago?

"How can this be? That would make you at least one hundred and ninety years old!" Adrian exclaimed.

"I gave up my wings to come here—to live amongst you. I wanted to experience the same emotions you do. If I had to do all over again, I would have made the choice again. Many of my friends and family I saw perish over my life here, but all of that means nothing now. My sole purpose is to protect you and guide you as far as I can to fulfilling the prophecy," Titus explained.

"Then answer this. If you were sent to protect me, where were you when I almost bought the farm back, there at that checkpoint?" Adrian asked.

"Just as Europhate explained to you in Amsterdam, you had to pass various tests before I could intervene. GOD gave you humans free will, it was your choices that allowed you to make it this far," Titus stated.

"Enough talk. Titus will answer any and all questions later. For now, you have training and time is of the essence," Europhate intervened. "Amelia, get food for our future warrior. He is going to need all of his strength."

May 2018

The room was brightly lit as he strolled in. The dark cherry lacquered furniture glistened from the sun's rays. Expensive décor was strategically placed throughout the office. As he walked to the desk, he graced the edge of the desk with his fingertips.

He smiled and sat behind the desk. Within minutes, two gentlemen walked into the room both showing concern on their faces.

"Sir, we have a problem," one of the men blurted out. "The task went aerie. One is dead, the other is in critical condition. He stated the chosen had a message for you. 'Your master, I am coming for him.' Seems he has chosen sides."

The distinguished man seemed disappointed but only for a brief minute or so. Then he smiled and looked at his two aides. He picked up the phone and pressed a few buttons.

"Everything is to go as planned. Schedule a meeting with the Joint Chiefs. We will convene at three o'clock." As he hung up the phone, he turned and looked at the aide who brought him the news. Within minutes, the aide's body convulsed as he collapsed to the floor. His body curled into a fetal position as the well-dressed executive walked from behind the desk.

"Nothing is written in stone. Man has free will and his will can be tested. Now what I want you to do is continue as planned. He will join or he will die by my hands if he doesn't."

The aide's body relaxed as if the force released him without warning. He coughed a couple of times as the other aide hesitantly walked over and helped his colleague to his feet.

"Now," the executive continued his statement, "get yourself cleaned and be ready and waiting in the meeting this afternoon. I have some matters I need to tend to."

The executive left the room and walked down the brightly lit hallway. He was nearly tackled by a beautiful secretary, her hair was done in a bun, the quintessential appearance of what most would consider as a high executive secretary would appear to look. Her business suit was without flaw as she stood almost the same height as the executive thanks to her stiletto-based heels that donned her feet.

She held on to the folders and papers in her hands as if her life depended on it.

"Sir, I received the information you needed, and you have your noon meeting with Congress. Also, your news conference is in twenty minutes. I also have your meeting you requested scheduled for the Joint Chiefs as you requested in the oval office."

The executive smiled. "Thank you, Janice. See to it that John is in attendance. Let him know I personally requested his presence."

Janice smiled, pulled out her cell, and dialed a few numbers. "Inform Sen. Greenhouse that his presence is requested for this afternoon's meeting with the Joint Chiefs in the oval office. Thank you."

She replaced her phone in her jacket lapel pocket and readdressed the executive. "Will there be anything else, sir?"

The executive smiled. "No, Janice, that will be all for now."

He walked out into the next office as reporters scampered with cameras and microphones trying to get any statements the executive could muster for the news of the day.

"Is it true you are running for president of the United States?" one of the reporters blurted.

"Yes, I feel our country is in disarray and we need powerful stances to put the threads back together that have unraveled our great country. The travesty that has befallen this nation is heart breaking, but as Americans, we must prevail. We have dealt with crisis and have overcame them many with unpopular reviews—Bush with the Gulf war; Clinton with economic reform; GW Bush with Iraq war; Obama with health care reform; and Nancy Grey in her efforts to bring about universal world peace. Her legacy will not go unnoticed. Her tireless efforts have given us as Americans a new sense of hope that there is a change in the air and that change is unity not only for these United States, but for the world. We must come together as one and unite around one concept. We are all equal, and that equality must be recognized by all, not just a select few. Let us spread to the world that equality must be obtained by all. Thank you, gentlemen."

The executive walked out of the room as the reporters clamored to get in more questions before he exited the room.

"Is this the next new leader for the United States? Can he be the new 'savior' in these trying times? Well, it seems the question has been answered with a definite YES. This is Sheryl Givens for CNN News."

The executive walked into the other room and closed the door. Within moments, the cell phone rang in his pocket. "Hello. Yes, it is in place. Yes, Father. He will join, I assure you. Greenhouse has no choice, he either joins or dies. And I believe his vanity will make the decision for him.

"Man's free will. It will be the downfall of the prophecy. How can he have so much love for a creature that spits in his face every chance they get? He will regret his favor for these dust molds! He will bow to you, Father, I will assure you of that.

"The soldier? I have that taken care of he will not live to see the end of his journey that I assure you."

Noon

The executive finished his lunch as Janice made her presence in the room. "Your twelve o'clock, sir?"

The executive smiled as he rose from the table and grabbed his jacket. Janice walked to him and made certain he was presentable as she aligned the jacket's lapel and brushed any foreign debris from his jacket. The executive kissed her on the cheek and walked out of the room with Janice sharply on his heels. They continued down the long hallway to a set of closed oak doors.

The executive walked in as cameras flashed like lightning in the calm before the storm. There was an eerie silence as the executive walked into the crowded room. Men of distinction sat on either side of the room. The confidence the executive exuded was undeniable. He made his way to the table before him and waited until he was addressed to be seated.

A voice boomed through the PA system as the executive patiently listened.

"We have gathered here for the past month to determine the successor to the presidency of these United States. The eyes of the world were focused on this occasion once before as we elected Barack Obama as president and once again as we elected Nancy Grey as the first female president. Now we are once again under the same microscope to determine the successor for the most precedent position any American could ever have. We the members of Congress are here to make our voices heard as to the selection of the next president.

"Due to circumstances that we all know to be rather unorthodox, we have amended into the constitution to allow by votes of the house and the senate the election of the president to continue the remaining term of the presidency held by the late Nancy Grey.

"However, on that note, we have been informed that the absentee vote for Sen. Greenhouse will be counted in these proceedings. So without further ado, House, what say you?"

The senior speaker for the House rose from his seat as he read the balloted votes. "We the House of Representatives voted respectfully 400 to 35 in favor of."

"Thank you. The Senate recognizes senior gentleman Rep. Josh Randolf. As I read off the ballots for the Senate, I would like to thank the men and women of congress in their diligent effort put into place in keeping our government in focus and upholding our constitutional values. The Senate concurs with the house with a 100 to 3 vote in favor of—ladies and gentlemen of congress, I would like to introduce to you the new president of these United States, Jonathan S. Lucian, the 45th President of the United States of America!"

There was a loud roar as the entire room thundered with applause. The executive smiled as he stood and made his way to the podium. He stood before the Chief Justice and placed his hand on the Bible.

His body began to twinge inside from the sting, but he fought the urge to pull his hand back.

"Sir, please repeat after me. I, Jonathan S. Lucian, do solemnly swear..."

"I, Jonathan S. Lucian, do solemnly swear..."

"That I will faithfully execute the office of the President of the United States, and will, to the best of my ability, preserve, protect, and defend the Constitution of the United States. So help me God."

"That I will faithfully execute the office of the President of the United States, and will, to the best of my ability, preserve, protect, and defend the Constitution of the United States. So help me God."

Upon the last phrase, the Bible let off a slight cinder as the cover left a burn mark. The Justice looked in fear as he quickly removed the Bible from under the executive's hand. He extended his hand. "Congratulations, Mr. President!"

The executive smiled as he shook the Justice's hand. "Thank you, sir."

The executive slowly turned to the podium and began to address Congress. "We as Americans have endured a terrible loss with the death of Nancy Grey. She was my mentor and friend; her legacy will forever endure. Now we must focus on a new chapter. A new era of democracy that will be universal and will be nothing short of a miracle. A democracy that will revolutionize the world as we know it and will bring about unity between warring nations, prosperity between poverty-stricken nations, and harmony between chaotic nations. We will unite Canada, Russia, China, Africa, and the Europe nations to work on one accord. To promote a universal peace we so desperately deserve."

There was a loud roar as the members of congress stood in an uplifting applause. He raised his hand to signal a silence amongst the crowd.

"We as a nation must lead by example. To show the world that we strive from adversity and that we prevail even when times were bleak. We have done this time and time again, with FDR, Reagan, Bush, GW Bush, Obama, and Grey. Now it is time for a new era.

"An era of change, an era of recognition, an era of revolution. These changes will not come overnight and certainly will not be met by all as the best solution. But we will meet each challenge with determination, with focus, and with an American grit and can-do spirit that we have carried with us for over four hundred years.

"This is our legacy, this is our focus, and this is our resolve as people of the United States of America! Thank you."

There was an enormous roar that ensued in the room as every person stood in applause to the statement of the new president as he waved his hands in the air for the support of the applause.

"Mr. President, you're needed in the oval office with the Joint Chiefs for briefing," Janice whispered into the executive's ear.

He nodded and followed his aide. The prophecy was in place, and he knew it as he smiled. He walked to the oval office as the secret service opened the doors for the new president.

The doors were closed behind him as he took his place among the table of the uniformed leaders.

"Gentlemen, the time has come for us to go forward. War is on the horizon and time is of the essence. We must begin to prepare for the threat that lies before us. Sen. Greenhouse, so good of you to join us."

Greenhouse nodded in recognition of the president's response. "I am honored to be here, Mr. President. I feel my life somewhat depended on it."

"Mr. President, what of these Bible-hugging believers that may be an opposition to our cause?"

The new president smiled. "Belief. There is always a lie in everyone. Don't worry about them. My father will make sure that my popularity will outweigh any belief that may be a threat to the cause. The NWO will be unstoppable. My father will make sure of that. You just focus on the soldier. He must be swayed by any cost."

"And if he does not agree to join?" one of the generals asked.

The president without missing a beat stated, "Kill him. That's all, gentlemen."

The aide that greeted the executive only moments earlier motioned to the new president. "Sir, he has arrived."

Jonathan smiled. "Show him to the office. I will be there momentarily. Senator, your help is needed. I am in need of your assistance in the persuasion of the ethics committee on your little deed. I have assigned a few people to your panel to help in this situation. Don't worry, you will not do any time, nor will you be executed for treason. You will be working undercover however with the NWO; I feel your presence will benefit us all—that is, if you are willing to accept the position."

The senator smiled and extended his hand. "As I stated earlier, it is as if my very life is dependent on this decision. You have my full support, Mr. President!"

Jonathan smiled. "I knew I could count on you. If you will excuse me, I have a prior engagement I must keep. You will be briefed on your objectives soon."

Jonathan left the room and returned to the presidential office. Standing before him was Vincent. The new president smiled. "Hello, Vincent. My father told me you were coming."

Vincent smiled. "Could never get Lucifer to keep a secret. Hello, Jonathan. You are definitely your father's child. Congratulations... not like you didn't know you would get the job. Let's cut to the chase. My time here is limited. I have news of the prophecy. He is growing stronger. He also has help. Titus and Europhate."

Jonathan looked shocked. "Titus? But Father told me he was dead? How can this be?"

Vincent shook his head in disagreement. "Seems he has been laying low all these years in preparation of the emergence of the soldier. Titus is a major threat. His skills are rivaled even amongst the angels. What do you suggest we do?"

Jonathan looked with concern. "Continue as planned. Man's greatest flaw is that of free will; he can be persuaded, it's just a matter of time."

Vincent laughed as Jonathan opened a box and removed a cigar. He rubbed his fingers as fire fizzled from the tips. He took two hard puffs and exhaled the smoke from the cigar.

Adrian sat in front of the television as he watched with concern of the event taking place back home.

"Jonathan S. Lucian as been voted in by congress as the 45th president of the United States. After an unprecedented and overwhelming vote of both the House and the Senate, the newly amended president was immediately rushed to his cabinet meeting with the Joint Chiefs to become briefed on the nation's current security affairs. Can this new president mend a nation torn with hate and despair? Only time will tell. Popularity will not win support, as did the last two presidents, he will have to show results to gain the trust of the American people. Back to you, Ted," the reporter announced.

Adrian looked at the still of the new president. It was something in him that made his flesh crawl. He knew something was not right with him, he could not figure out how or why.

Titus walked in and sat next to Adrian. "Do not doubt your feelings, you should feel concerned."

Adrian looked toward Titus. "Is that the—"

"Anti-Christ," Titus finished the statement. "He has been placed in office, now the prophecy begins. As I stated before, we have little time. You must be ready to train; nothing can be taken for granted. He is a formable foe, and he is very strong. But there is one thing you have that he doesn't."

"What's that?" Adrian asked.

Titus smiled. "Me! Now get yourself ready, we have more training to do."

Titus took Adrian to a room. He tapped the wall three times as an unusual symbol appeared on the wall. There was a bright light that seemed to grow within seconds it consumed the wall.

"Come, Adrian," Titus commanded.

The two walked through the light and proceeded along the illuminated path. The entire dimension seemed mystical as the two continued down the path.

Adrian was experiencing that peace he felt when his wife visited him in the garden. He felt relieved. At the end of the tunnel, he saw silhouettes of seven forms seated before him. Each form slowly stood, and their wings expanded in all their glory and beauty. On the table before them sat seven bowls and seven trumpets.

"Standing before you, Adrian, are the ultimate warriors of heaven and earth. You will be bestowed from each a gift. Use these gifts wisely, Adrian, for you will be forever tempted by Lucifer himself. Free will has been a blessing for man but also a curse. Stay forever faithful and diligent to what is right and true. All men have and will falter, but it is up to man to redeem himself," Titus exclaimed.

There was a loud rush of air as each angel bestowed upon Adrian their distinct gift.

Titus called out each gift as it manifested itself into Adrian's body and soul.

"God's Holy Armor to protect the flesh and enrich the soul; the sword of truth to battle the darkness and aid in doubt and confusion; the Piercing of the Soul to cleanse the possessed and banish the demons within; the Prophecy of Megiddo, the guiding force to the final battle, this will be your map and your warning tool in times of danger; Gabriel's Trumpet, this will be used to call the armies of GOD during the final battle, use this well, for it will help you in your most trying times; the True Shroud of Christ to aid in healing yourself and others around you; Wings of Truth to use as a shroud to encase you in times of rest and rejuvenation; God's Fury allows rain of fire and brimstone upon your foe; and finally, my gift to you, the Medallion of the Righteous, this has endured over four hundred years of trial and tribulations, it bestows the hardship of the American Indians, the suffering of the slaves, the persecution of the Jews, the injustice of the people of Africa and China, and the enslavement of the Israelites. You will learn most from this medallion for it will feed off your compassion and aid you in hard times and will give you enlightenment. Keep this close to your heart, Adrian, this can be the difference between success and failure."

Adrian's body rose from the enlightened path as the gifts took form; from his back, wings were exposed and began to spread. Angelic voices rejoiced in song as Adrian's body was encased with the gifts bestowed to him. He blew into Gabriel's trumpet as he announced his presence. He was ready to fulfill his destiny. As he blew, legions of angels flew overhead awaiting his call for the last battle. He knew his destiny was paved and his journey, his true journey was about to begin. It was time.

Adrian opened his eyes as he got out of the bed. He looked around the room and smiled. He knew what had happened and felt confident in his journey and what he was chosen to do. Amelia stood in the doorway to his room.

"You're awake. I'm glad. Titus sent me to inform you it is time to leave," Amelia stated.

Adrian nodded his head in agreement; he knew it was time to fulfill his destiny. Now the true test begins.

Chapter 6: Revisited

Adrian, Titus, and Amelia got in the car. Titus stated they must go back to the United States. But first one thing must be taken care of by Amelia before she could rejoin her parents. As Titus drove, Adrian and Amelia engaged in conversation and silly traveling games. Adrian felt as if he were living his life with his family through Amelia. He held to his vow of protecting Amelia even if his life depended on it. He never imagined he would grow as close as he had with Amelia and now the vow has become more personal than ever. They traveled for three days without incident.

Each enjoying the trip and each other's company. Titus dazzled them with stories of his time on earth. The people he met and the things he accomplished during his time. Adrian was fascinated by his stories of the migration to the north, the Jim Crow laws from the south, and the chaos of the fifties and sixties. He spoke of the wars he fought in World Wars 1 and 2 and the many comrades he buried along the way. The conflicts he encountered of being accepted over in the states after the war. He explained why he moved to Europe amidst the chaos that ensued in the sixties. He found that people were more accepting of him in Europe than in the states. However, the prejudices were still encountered here; they were not as pronounced as he had encountered state side.

Adrian was somewhat disappointed. "How did you keep from losing it and going ballistic on someone?"

Titus smiled. "I did what anyone with faith would do. I prayed." They stayed the night in a safe house along the way. Titus taught Adrian how to recognize a safe house just as he did in the years of the

Underground Railroad. Each safe house will have on its porch a lantern—lit means it is safe to stop; if it was not lit, it means stay away, there is danger nearby and to continue to the next station.

The trio slept well and arose early to proceed to their destination. As they began to drive along the long stretch of road, almost immediately, Titus came to an abrupt stop.

"Amelia, stay put. When I tell you to, I want you to take the car and continue to Geneva. We will meet you there. Do you understand me, Amelia? No matter what, do not stop for anything."

Amelia agreed with fear in her eyes.

"Come, Adrian. We have work to do," Titus commanded.

Adrian exited the car and followed Titus into the woods for three miles until they reached a clearing. Titus stopped. He sniffed the air several times and smiled.

"Hello, Vincent," Titus stated softly.

"Titus! I am truly surprised to see you. I thought you were dead," Vincent exclaimed. He emerged from behind a tree just east of their position.

"No, I am alive and well. What brings you here, Vincent?" Titus replied.

"Now you know very well why I am here. Adrian cannot continue. You know that these dust molders do not deserve his favor. What can these dusties do? Cause war, confusion, hatred amongst their own kind? Ain't that right, porch monkey!" Vincent stated as he looked at Adrian.

Adrian could feel the blood boil in his veins. Titus looked at Adrian and smiled. "Do not let him get to you," he whispered.

"Vincent, why must you allow your jealousy rule your thoughts? You know GOD has never forgotten us, he has always cherished us. Must you follow the same path as Lucifer?"

"Silas was smart!" Vincent screamed. "He saw what he was doing and how he loved man more than us. He even sacrificed his own son for these dusties! Do you think he would have done it for us? They don't deserve his grace, his favor, and his love! They don't even care for self as they commit suicide when nothing goes their way or murder each other out of lust, greed, or hatred, let alone abiding by his word or any kind of prophecy! Why would you protect that? How can you love that?"

Titus smiled as he listened to Vincent's rants. He knew Vincent was right on all accounts, but there was one thing Titus could attest to that Vincent couldn't.

"Vincent, all you have said is true. However, there is one thing I can say on their behalf that you will never know firsthand. Through all their faults, they share something that you could never grasp and that took me over four hundred years to understand. They have faith. They are faced with the most severe of situations, but they have faith that GOD will see them through. They don't expect it to be resolved at times just to make it to the other side of the trouble that lay before them. This is what makes them different from you and me. They hold on to faith and that is stronger than anything we could ever imagine."

Enraged, Vincent screamed as a large blast of light flowed from his hands toward Titus. Titus was blown ten feet across the clearing. Three other demons emerged from above heading straight to Adrian. Adrian immediately focused on the first one as his eyes turned blood red, the demon stopped in midair and exploded before reaching him. Adrian then turned to greet the other demon; he raised his arm in toward the heavens as a sword appeared in his hand. As he came down with the sword in hand, he severed the demon's head in one swoop.

The third demon retreated to Vincent perched and ready to strike.

"Seems you are stronger than I thought, Adrian," Vincent exclaimed.

"You have no idea, Vincent. And it is funny I really trusted you," Adrian stated as he advanced toward Vincent.

Vincent stopped the blade by clasping the sides with both hands.

"As I stated earlier, be careful who you trust." He pushes Adrian's advancement away. Adrian fell to the ground but bounced up almost instantly. Before Adrian could advance again, Titus grabbed his shoulder.

"No, Vincent is mine. Get back to the car and protect Amelia. Remember your promise!" Titus screamed.

Adrian nodded and headed back to Amelia. Vincent looked toward the demon. Almost instantly, the demon took to flight. With the speed of the wind, he raced to where Amelia sat. Adrian ran as fast as his legs could take him shouting along the way, "Amelia, get the hell out of here! Amelia, go now!"

Amelia, hearing Adrian's shouts, obeyed him. She started the car and placed it in drive. Just as she was driving off, the demon landed on the roof of the car. She swerved violently to force the demon's grasp loose but to no avail. Adrian screamed as the wings appeared from his flesh, he took flight after the two, and within minutes, he landed on the demon and forced loose his grip as the two fell to the ground. Adrian raised his had to the air again as the sword appeared once more.

The demon walked in a small circle preparing for the battle ahead. Adrian felt no compassion, no remorse; he knew he had to save Amelia no matter what. Adrian began to advance toward the demon.

The demon smiled and vanished and almost instantly appeared behind Adrian with Amelia in grasp.

He smiled as he severed Amelia's jugular in effortless motion. Adrian screamed as he ran toward the demon. Adrian turned a glowing solid white as he screamed. A powerful light came from his mouth and eyes as he burned the demon to a cinder. Adrian fell to the ground; he felt exhausted but only for a moment or two. He walked over to Amelia's body and fell to his knees. He placed his hands gently across his bleeding neck. A soft and gentle light glistened from his hands as the wound closed. Amelia opened her eyes and smiled. "We are even now," she whispered. Adrian smiled and helped her into the car as they turned back to get Titus.

Titus and Vincent were still fighting. Titus lunged as Vincent saw his advance and countered. They clashed in midair. The sheer impact caused a loud shudder that sounded like thunder during a violent storm.

"Your jealousy will be the death of you, Vincent," Titus screamed as he cut Vincent deeply with a small dagger.

Vincent screamed and disengaged from Titus's grasp. Vincent looked at Titus and smiled as he took wings and flew away in the distance.

"This is not over, Vincent," Titus exclaimed. "It is far from over."

Adrian and Amelia arrived shortly afterward. "Titus! You all right?"

Titus turned toward the voice. "Yes, Adrian, I am fine. Seems you brought with you a very disobedient child." Titus smiled.

"Well, you can fault me for that, seems the demons wanted to cause harm to Amelia."

"Well, she is safe now and that is all that matters. Let us get her to Geneva so she can get back to her parents. Shall we?" Titus asked as he pointed back to the direction of the car.

The three made it to Geneva without further incident. They pulled into a safe house and knocked on the door. Before them stood Marek. "What took you guys so damn long? I was beginning to worry."

"We ran into some old friends of yours. It seems Vincent is back, and he is not very happy, I might add," Titus explained.

"Man, you fucking angels just don't know when to stay gone, do you?" Marek laughed.

Titus had to find that funny as he joined Marek in laughter.

That Evening

They sat at the table as Amelia laid out the map of Megiddo; she closed her eyes as the map let out a faint glow in the dimly lit room.

"Here is the path the armies will gather, the arc will be positioned here. Adrian, you must not falter, your presence with the arc is crucial. He will try to stop you by any and all means, so you must be on your toes at all times," Amelia exclaimed.

Adrian listened intently.

"You will need to be prepared for I will be joining my brothers here real soon to begin the release of the remaining seals. You ready?" Marek asked.

"I have to be whether I am or not. This is my destiny, it must be fulfilled," Adrian answered.

"Then it's settled," Titus exclaimed. "Thank you, Amelia. Marek, see that Amelia gets back to her family safely."

Marek nodded in agreement as he escorted Amelia out. Before walking out of the door, he turned and addressed Titus. "I will meet you two in Houston. It would be safer than flying directly to DC."

Adrian ran outside to meet Amelia. "Hey, kid, you take care of yourself. No crazy stunts here?"

Amelia smiled and ran to embrace Adrian. "Take care as well, Adrian. I don't want hear about you dying on me, okay?"

"I promise," Adrian stated.

Marek shook Adrian's hand and left with Amelia. Adrian stood in the drive until he could no longer see the taillights of the car. He walked back in as Titus stood over the map.

"Smile, Adrian, you will see her again," Titus stated without looking up from the map. "Go and rest, we have an early day tomorrow."

Adrian took Titus's advice and headed to the bedroom. He lay across the bed as he stared at the ceiling. He thought back on the conversation he and Amelia shared just days earlier. The traveling games they played along the way. Then he thought about the attack from the demon and his ability to save Amelia's life. He smiled as he envisioned her smiling face as she opened her eyes as she lay in his arms.

"I guess we are even, Amelia," he stated as he smiled and turned over on his side as he drifted off to sleep.

The Next Morning

Adrian and Titus checked their luggage at the airport in Geneva. Titus left to get the tickets as Adrian stopped at the small coffee shop to grab coffee for him and Titus. He made the purchase and walked back to the counter. Titus and Adrian grabbed a seat as they waited for their flight to board. Adrian learned a lot about Titus; he too was in love and had a family, but they were killed while they tried to escape to Canada. His child was no more than two. Klansmen raided a safe house and killed the family that aided them to escape.

He was unable to get to his wife and child in time due to some problems with the fake papers given to him prior to leaving. When he learned of his family's fate, he was filled with rage and anger. But he was able to channel that anger to helping others escape.

He joined forces at times with Harriet Tubman to guide many slaves to freedom. He never married again. He refused to get close to anyone after that in fear it would cause the same travesty that fell upon him. He felt deep down that Adrian was his second chance and treated him like a son. He chose to do so to make up for the inability to protect his own family. He could see much of himself in Adrian for they shared the same fate but also shared the same humanity.

They both refused to let the hate consume them and to use the hate to channel the love they had for self and humanity.

They had to live their family's redemption through their own lives. To honor the sacrifice made by them properly. The call to board was made as the two walked with the crowd like cattle waiting to be branded. They searched for their seat and placed their belongings in the overhead compartment. The flight was long, but they realized the two had more in common than they thought.

Titus gave up his wings to come to earth to fulfill the prophecy. He fell in love and married a slave by the name of Elizabeth. She was beautiful, timid, and caring. Titus began to obtain a lot of human emotions and could not bear to see her mistreated.

Titus found the master forcing himself on her. When she refused, he beat her until she gave in. Titus, filled with rage, wanted revenge, but he knew vengeance was not his. He aided her and his child's escape from the plantation. They were administered false papers. Elizabeth and the babies were fine, but Titus knew his would not pass. He encouraged her to continue without him and he would join them very soon.

Titus was led off by Harriet, while Elizabeth and his child waited to make their escape. They had made it to the second station, to stop and rest while venturing north to freedom. Elizabeth and the others were asleep in the secret room in the loft when a group of slave hunters stormed the house killing the homeowners and two slaves, Elizabeth and her child. It was said they killed her because she fought back. Titus never married again and kept her and his child's memory in his heart forever. He knew when his work was done, he would join them, so he stayed vigilant.

Adrian felt renewed after hearing Titus's story. Here was a man who had endured for over 190 years and his love for her had never faltered.

Mallory's Visit

Marek drove down I-10 to the Heights area on the northern part of Houston. He exited the freeway and continued down the feeder road to a narrow street off set from the feeder. He turned right and maneuvered his car down the narrow alley where he came to a stop. He exited the car and walked to the door of what looked to be an abandoned building. He knocked three times as a man looked through a sliding peep door. He looked at Marek and smiled as he opened the door.

"Marek. Glad you could make it," the man stated.

"Good evening, Governor. Is everything in order?" Marek greeted.

"Yes. We are ready. The shipment can take place tonight."

"Good. Has Vincent been by as I expected?" Marek asked.

"Yes. We informed him the warrior will be here but have not disclosed any other information," the man stated.

"Good. Well, let me get to the airport, can't keep our guest waiting, now, can we?" Marek stated.

They arrived in Houston Bush Intercontinental Airport. Titus retrieved their luggage while Adrian went in search for Mallory. Adrian walked to the upper-ground level when he spotted Mallory.

"How was the trip?" Marek asked.

"Too damn long!" Adrian laughed in reply.

The two met up with Titus and aided with the luggage.

"I have good news. I have found the arc of the covenant," Marek stated. "Seems religious groups named the Knights of the Righteous Order have had it here in the states since WWII. When Germany invaded Poland, Hitler's focus was to obtain the arc. Seems he had read the Bible too," Marek joked.

"Any army that has the arc before it shall not be defeated. So how did it get here?" Titus asked.

Marek explained, "When Poland was invaded, the arc was located in a vault located under a church there. When news of Hitler's plot was revealed, the knights made it their mission to relocate the arc to prevent Hitler from obtaining it. They smuggled it into the states where it has been since 1942. Seems they have been following the prophecy as well, and they know the first seal is about to be broken. We are to meet up with them this evening."

"Where is it being kept?" Adrian asked.

"Have you ever heard of the saying never let the right hand know what the left one is doing? Well, it seems that they arc is located in Iron Mountain located in Colorado," Marek stated, smiling.

"Iron Mountain? You mean to tell me the same people that shred and keep old documents have been having the arc all this time and no one has known about it, not even the government?" Adrian asked.

"It is hard to believe, but yeah. I guess if you don't want anything found, put it right under someone's nose! We will meet this evening. I reserved my brother's private jet to get us to Colorado; I just can't seem to fathom having to check the arc in baggage. That would be right rude, would you not agree?" Marek stated.

Adrian was rather amused with Marek's sense of humor. It felt good to make light of the issue. It allowed him to keep in touch with his humanity. Something he had been holding on to throughout his journey.

Hours later, they met up with their contact; they drove to a private airstrip somewhere in Sugarland as he bordered Mallory's jet en route to Colorado to fulfill the prophecy.

That Evening

Jonathan walked into the dining area where Vincent sat waiting.

"Well, it is more of how I can help you," Vincent replied. "It seems your adversary has come back to the states. I thought you may want to see your competition," Vincent stated as he grimaced with pain.

"He did that to you?" Jonathan asked.

"No, my dear friend Titus is fighting alongside him. It seems the warrior has received a protector as well," Vincent answered.

"Well, I must formally introduce myself to him. You will be revenged, Vincent, don't worry. Where has our 'prophecy' been spotted?" Jonathan asked.

"Word has it somewhere in Houston. Word has not spread here about my allegiance, so a few of the knights still trust me enough to supply some information. Although, they would not say why he was here... which I find that to be rather odd. If you know you are the chosen, why would you come back to harm's way?" Vincent questioned.

"Well, let me ask him myself; I feel it would be very poor manners not to introduce myself to my opponent," Jonathan stated.

"Janice, schedule a trip to Houston. I need to visit an old friend there anyway," Jonathan requested.

"Yes, Mr. President," she replied.

Two Hours Later

Mallory's plane touched down on a private strip. It taxied to an abandoned hangar where two men stood waiting. The plane came to a stop as the pilot and the contact exited the plane. The cargo door was opened, and the crate was loaded onto the plane. Marek waved from the window. The contact stayed behind as he shook the pilot's hand and left with the other two men.

The pilot got back on the plane, and they taxied back to the runway and within minutes were airborne.

Marek viewed into the crate. It was the arc securely packed. "I will get you guys back to Houston. My driver will take you back to Mallory's. Make yourselves at home. I will get this to Megiddo. I will be expecting you guys back in there within a few days. Be very careful here, my brother will make his ride here very soon; the second seal is soon to be broken."

Titus and Adrian agreed. Adrian knew the real reason he was here and that was to see the Anti-Christ for himself. He felt anxious as if this was to be the final battle. He knew that was yet to come, but he felt ready to take him on at that moment. Hours later, Adrian and Titus were on the ground in Sugarland as the crate was unloaded and loaded on a much-larger plane. Marek bid them farewell and boarded the larger. Adrian and Titus watched as the plane taxied to the runway and watched it as it took off.

"Let's go, I have a feeling you will have a visitor to meet tomorrow," Titus stated.

"I am looking forward to it," Adrian exclaimed.

Chapter 7: The Battle Has Begun

The 2nd Seal

The angels wept when the rider paraded before them. The pale spotted horse seemed disoriented and despondent. The horse pounded the ground; rot and decay formed from each mark his hoof made upon the soil. The thick stagnant mist from his nostrils filled the air with a foul sulfurous stench.

The rider looked to either side of him as the angels made every attempt not to look into his eyes; for within his dark cold eyes gave a despairing glimmer of plague and disease. He knew he would be the ailment that would plague humanity, the infection of hate and discontent. He mounted his horse; the beast pulled the reigns in resistance from its owner. The rider grabbed the mane and yanked with malice. He gave an evil snicker, grunted, and quickly regained control of the beast.

With an ungodly wail, the beast reared as the rider gave an unsettling laugh. The beast galloped along steadily as it approached Matthew. Matthew looked back and cringed; the second rider had emerged. Marlon glared at his brother with hate and anger, his beast spewed a mist from his nostrils that that blanketed the air with a foul thick smog of death and rotted flesh.

The second seal was broken.

Friday, February 2029

Chaos had truly ensued. Confusion took hold of the human race as disease and famine ran rampant throughout the world. Religious groups tried uniting as one, while radical groups chose various sides to determine the final battle. Many others were confused on whom they should attach their allegiance. Uncertain as to who was right or wrong, extremist groups that did not follow the code were executed.

The anti-Christ obtained power and people were swayed by his influence. Jonathan began his term of office in Ohio, swaying political influences by providing more social and economic change for the middle-class families and increasing programs for the poor.

He knew by winning over the people's confidence by giving them want they wanted in the time they needed it the most, the election process would be easily obtained. Jonathan bridged the gap between Afghanistan and US relations and developed a ceasefire and eventually a treaty established between Israeli and Muslim relations. The people of the US felt he was the answer for all their problems. Secretly, Jonathan used the NWO-gained momentum as they established dominance through fear. With their political backing and rhetoric of fear and hate, religious groups who once feared God were now using God to instill fear in others.

The Order used terroristic tactics to bring about social change and hid behind God to make their agenda believable. Catholics, Christians, Muslims, Jehovah's Witness, all these multiple religions were becoming no more as religion has now gone underground. Fear struck the once free society.

Adrian went into the kitchen. He could not sleep. Something was bothering him, and he could not figure out what. He opened the fridge and looked at its contents. Marek's brother Marlon was somewhat of a health nut, which is somewhat ironic being he was the horseman of Famine.

Adrian chuckled at the thought, as he grabbed some fruit from the fridge and walked back to the living room. He grabbed the remote and started flipping the channel. He stopped on a national news channel to see what he had missed for the past few months.

"President Jonathan L. Ahriman III will be in Houston meeting with Sen. Olson and Gov. Green as they talk about the economic impact the new financial treaty passed by the new United Front, a subsidiary of the United Nations. If talks are successful, Houston could see an increase in revenue and will make it an economic power city rivaling the likes of New York, San Francisco, and Los Angeles combined. Although sources speculate that this could be the beginning of the end of the currency as we know it. Some religious groups state it is the mark of the beast, if you believe in that sort of thing. This is Stephanie Lakes, KHOU Eleven News, this morning."

Adrian paused the DVR to focus on the new president's face. He felt the blood rushing through his veins. "This is the anti-Christ," he huffed. "I need to go the airport now. NOW!"

Titus walked into the room. "You will have your chance but not now."

"I want to see him for myself. No TV, no photo, I want to see him in person."

"As you wish. Get dressed. We can have the driver take us to the airport. You will get your wish, all I ask in return is you restrain yourself. Now is not the time to fight."

Adrian reluctantly gave his word as he veered back toward his image again. It is time to size up his enemy.

Later That Morning

Jonathan's plane landed in Houston the following morning. He waited onboard as he continued his conference call.

"I don't give a damn! They will obey or be destroyed. Send troops there. If they can't accept my terms, we will provide other means of persuasion," he boomed.

"Mr. President, we have arrived," the pilot announced over the PA system.

Jonathan smiled. He stood and looked himself over as Janice reached for his coat. She helped him put it on and brushed away any foreign material. Jonathan thanked her and exited the plane.

People greeted him with cheers and applause as he strutted down the makeshift stairway. Secret Service men swarmed around him as he waved and greeted the crowd.

"Mr. President, Senator Olson and Governor Green are here to meet with you," Janice whispered.

"Thank you, Janice. Set us up in a conference room for noon," he commanded.

"Yes, Mr. President," Janice replied.

News media swarmed him as cameras flashed like lightning, streaking across the sky aiming at the president. With a smile, he waved to the crowd.

One pushy reporter bogarted his way to the front. "Mr. President. Mr. President. Can you give a statement? The economic status is unreal. Prosperity is more abundant now than it has been in years. The new currency seems to be global. What's your next agenda, and how will it affect the citizens both here and abroad?"

Jonathan smiled. "America has been faced with many obstacles and we have met the challenges head on. Now we are faced with countries that wish to threaten our way of life. As your president, it is my responsibility to rid our country of any such threats whether foreign or domestic. Our country is the greatest in the world, and it is up to us to lead by example, and it is my duty that we do just that. Thank you, no more questions."

"Good answer," Janice whispered.

"Thank you. This should get the people on board for the invasion." Jonathan gave a compassionate smile. He was glad he was able to add some comfort to a stressful situation.

As he looked to the crowd, he saw a man staring at him. He knew from the stare that it must be the warrior for which the prophecy foretold.

Adrian looked at him with a sense of hate. The same emotions that filled him during his family's death seemed to build in him from the sheer sight of Jonathan.

His body ached because he wanted to go after him and end it right then and there. But he knew he would be killed by his secret service before he even got to him. Jonathan looked at Adrian with an arrogant grin, and with a mocking gesture, he waved at Adrian and disappeared into the crowd on the tarmac.

"Come, Adrian, you will have your chance," Titus proclaimed.

Jonathan was escorted to the presidential caravan. He stepped into The Beast along with Janice.

He made himself comfortable while Janice began handing him folders with various papers she needed his approval on.

He glanced over the items in each folder and showed his approval and recommendations needed for each with a scribble from his pen. Upon completion,, Janice addressed his agenda for the day.

"You have a meeting with the governor and senator and a brunch following the meeting. You also have a campaign meeting with the governor for the November election."

"Have you received word from Vincent about tonight's events?" Jonathan asked.

"Yes, it is scheduled. Your father has taken the necessary precautions," Janice replied.

"Father was always one for details. Let my father know I wish to attend. I want to see just what is so special about this 'warrior,'" Jonathan replied.

"Yes, Mr. President," Janice replied.

"Janice, why so formal?" Jonathan asked.

"I'm trying to be professional. I don't want to mix business with pleasure," Janice replied in a coy manner.

"Noted. However, I am the president, so what I say goes," Jonathan replied. With that, he grabbed Janice, and the two embraced in a passionate kiss as the caravan continued to its destination.

Marek woke from his nap. They were still in flight to Megiddo. He reached for his cell and dialed a preprogrammed number. There was a short silence as the phone rang.

"Marek, have you arrived safely?" the voice on the other end asked.

"No, we are still a few hours away. Has the announcement been made? Are they putting aside their differences to unite?" Marek asked.

"It is coming along. The Christians and the Muslims are finally coming together. The others will fall into place soon enough. Time is running out. I don't know if we will be able to assemble in enough time."

Marek interrupted the man's concern. "Don't worry. They'll come around. Remember, you must have faith." Marek noticed that was weird coming from his mouth. He of all people had the nerve to try to encourage someone to have faith. He smiled as he disconnected the call. He could not help thinking of his daughters as he reflected on the comment he had made earlier. "Just have faith," he whispered.

The Meeting

Jonathan arrived in the room with the Joint Chiefs. As he scoped the room, he saw Vincent seated with a not-so-happy expression on his face. Jonathan knew something was not right.

"We have a problem. The arc has been recovered and is on its way to Megiddo. It had been here the whole time!" Vincent blurted.

Jonathan was floored by the news. How could this be? The ultimate weapon was right under their noses, and no one was the wiser.

"You useless sons of bitches! You can't complete one simple task? Get the fuck out! All of you, get the fuck out!" Jonathan screamed.

Everyone left the room except for Vincent. He stayed put as he stared at Jonathan.

"I want revenge. I want to repay Titus for the injuries I received by his hand. Let me join you," Vincent requested.

"No..." Jonathan decided against the idea at first but then figured it would be beneficial if Vincent did join the raid. "Yes, Vincent. You will have your revenge. I will see to it personally," Jonathan replied.

There was a knock on the door as Janice entered the room.

"Mr. President, your father is here," she replied.

"Send him in."

Lucifer entered the room and positioned himself at the head of the conference table. "Your legion is ready for battle. Do you need me to assist?" Lucifer stated in an arrogant manner.

"No, Father, this one I need to do on my own. I guess you are aware of the arc. What do we do now? We are defenseless against them?"

Lucifer became enraged. "Shut up! I refuse to believe that some oversized box will defeat my minion. I will not allow it to. Man and their foolish beliefs! And you of all people falling for a myth! If it was so mighty, why didn't he keep it for himself instead of entrusting it to some dusties? Don't be fooled, son. GOD has more to fear from us. YOU HEAR ME, YOU SON OF A BITCH! I WILL WIN!" he shouted toward the heavens.

"Now you will meet this warrior and you will kill him and end this prophecy bullshit once and for all. And you know why I know this? Because you are my son and your dominion can be rivaled by no one," Lucifer stated as he slowly edged his way over and placed his hand on his son's shoulder.

"I will, Father. Rest assured I will," Jonathan replied.

Later That Evening

Adrian and Titus trekked the manicured gardens at Marek's estate. Titus explained the tasks that Adrian would be encountering upon the return to Megiddo.

Titus stopped as he motioned for Adrian to stay. Something was not right. It fell silent in an unsettling way.

"On your guard, Adrian," Titus shouted.

Without warning, demons came from every direction as they surrounded the two. The skies grew ominously black as Vincent descended from above. Shortly the demons parted their ring that surrounded Adrian and Titus as Jonathan approached with an arrogant swagger toward the two.

"Hello, warrior. My, my, my... GOD is really scraping the barrel; he has not one but two niggers to do his work for him. Ah, he was always for affirmative action, ain't that right, boy!" he stated as he directed his comment toward Titus.

"You would know. He made us in his image. Oh, I'm sorry, you are your father's child. I surely hate that for you," Titus replied.

"You dare mock my father? You are definitely defiant. Didn't you learn enough from the whippings you received on the plantation, boy? You gave up your wings to be humiliated, beaten, scorned, and for his sake, be a nigger. I'd say you got the raw end of the deal, wouldn't you, Vincent?" Jonathan replied.

Vincent laughed. "Let me handle this. You have a more pressing battle to take on."

"I agree but first I want to see just how good this 'warrior' is. Shall we?" Jonathan boasted, and without warning, his eyes turned black as death. He stared at Adrian and, with tremendous force, threw Adrian across the yard. Adrian slowly got to his feet.

"Is that all you got, you half-ass wannabe bigot?" Adrian screamed as he called forth his sword and slashed through the demons standing before him.

He charged toward Jonathan and, with one swoop, sliced Jonathan across his stomach.

Jonathan screamed in agony when Vincent instructed the demons to surround Jonathan for protection. Jonathan was escorted from the battle as Vincent and Titus squared away again in battle.

Demons were attacking from every direction as Adrian tried to fend as many off as he could.

"Adrian, quickly call for the trumpet!" Titus screamed.

Adrian summoned the trumpet, and with one blow, a loud bugled sound flowed from it. Within seconds, the seven angels appeared. The first angel raised her hands in a slow and graceful manner; the skies turned reddish black tint as the clouds rolled away like a scroll as summoned GOD's Fury. Cyclone funnels of fire targeted the demons burning them to a cinder and laid waste to the multiple demons surrounding Adrian. The second angel summoned a wind so severe that it cut through the remaining demons with razor-sharp precision. Vincent and Titus were deadlocked, each suffering their battle wounds. Vincent, looking around, noticed he was the only one left, glanced at his wounds, and smiled.

"Until next time, Titus," Vincent exclaimed as he forced his wings to spread and he flew off into the night. Almost instantly, the sky cleared into a starry night.

Adrian ran to help Titus. He was hurt pretty bad, but he would live. Adrian used the shroud to heal Titus.

"You did well, Adrian. We must go."

"No. Not until you are healed," Adrian exclaimed.

"Thanks." Titus smiled.

Adrian smiled back as he helped his friend back into the house. He made sure Titus was comfortable in the guest room as he closed the door. Adrian walked into the study and grabbed the phone. He dialed and waited for the phone to be answered.

"Marek, we need to leave here now," Adrian blurted.

"What's wrong? Are you guys all right?" Marek commanded.

"Yeah. We had a run in with the new president," Adrian answered.

"Jonathan? Did Sil—I mean his father come?" Marek corrected himself quickly.

"Vincent was here, and he hurt Titus pretty bad. He's resting now. Who is Jonathan's father?"

"What the fuck you mean 'Who is Jonathan's father'? You don't read much, do you? Man, you are just like Marc, don't pay attention to shit! Lucifer. Did Lucifer show?" Marek stated rudely.

"Yo, man, I had no idea and you don't have to be all funny with people," Adrian snapped back.

"Get the fuck out of your feelings, Adrian... we don't have time for it. Now pay close attention 'cause I will only say this once. Jonathan is not someone you wanna fuck with. You may be strong, but not strong enough to contend with the likes of him. Now once Titus is well enough to travel, you two get your asses back to Amsterdam. I will send for you later. It will be safer in Amsterdam because it would be the last place they would look for you. Use what was given to you by the seven and get Titus healed and out of there," Marek instructed.

"But what about the damages that were done in the garden?" Adrian asked.

"Man, fuck that house, that's material shit... it can be replaced. I'll handle it, my brother will understand, and if he don't... ,well it is like a cold, he will get over it; you just do what I told you to do. I will send for you two soon. Tell Titus to be careful. Vincent is out for blood and won't be happy until he gets it," Marek replied.

Marek hung up the phone. He knew he had to continue with the plan. He could not alter it in any way. He was in battle mode and had to think fast.

"I refuse to lose them both. Not on my watch," he thought.

Regret

"No! No!" Jonathan shouted. His anger resonated throughout the room. He gave an evil look to the people in the room.

"How is it you have been beaten twice by a dusty? A fuckin' DUSTY!" he screamed.

"Father would not be happy behind this. And you of all people should have known better," he stated as he glared at Vincent. He was even more disappointed with him than anyone in the room. He set up the opportunity for Vincent to get his revenge and he failed.

"I hope you enjoyed yourself?" Jonathan commented.

"I got my revenge! Titus can't help someone if he is wounded himself. Besides if you want to kill the warrior, go kill him your damn self!" Vincent screamed.

"I plan on it," Jonathan replied as he walked out of the door. Secret service scurried to escort the president to The Beast.

"No, not today, men, I need to be alone. I will be fine," Jonathan commented.

One of the secret service men interjected, "But, sir—"

"Damn it, I'm fine!" Jonathan shouted.

He motioned the valet as a black Mercedes silently rolled into view. Jonathan got in the car and drove out of the hotel garage. He was destined to kill Adrian. There was no need in keeping a prophecy alive. It had to end, for his father's sake.

Adrian went into the guest room to help Titus. He used the gift bestowed upon him, the shroud of healing, to take care of Titus's wounds. Adrian informed Marek's butler to drive them to the airport. After they left, Adrian replayed the instructions given to him by Marek. Marek wasn't the nicest person he ever met, but he knew he had his best interest in mind and that was enough for him.

The butler was driving like he was running from the law. Adrian knew the urgency of getting out of the states, so he did not criticize the driver of his erratic driving skills. They made it to the airport.

Adrian purchased the two tickets and checked the luggage while Titus tried to gather his strength. Within an hour, they were airborne and headed back to Amsterdam. Adrian knew he had not seen the last of Jonathan and he was definitely looking forward to their next confrontation.

After what seemed like forever, Jonathan drove into Marek's estate. Jonathan parked the car and exited with caution. He walked through the house in hopes of finding his rival, but to his dismay, they were not there.

He exited the house to the garden and viewed the damage his small crew had caused. Pissed, he trashed what he could of the place and left.

I should've stayed. I should've stayed and fought, he thought.

"No, my son," a voice chimed in the wind.

"Why not, Father? I could have killed him right there in that fuckin' garden. He was no match for me! Fuck him, fuck Titus, fuck GOD! We will not bow to that arrogant son of a bitch, not him... not his son... Fuck both of them!"

"Calm yourself, son, we will get them soon, but for now, don't worry about it. The time will come. I assure you. As for now, leave this place, I have bigger things for you to do."

Jonathan smirked as he obeyed his father's wish. He snapped his fingers as the house burst into flames. He walked through the flames as if it was a mere mist; his clothes reeked of burning ember but not a single thread of his clothing was singed. He glanced back and the place exploded.

He laughed as he opened the door to his Mercedes. Pleased with himself, he adjusted the rearview mirror so that he could enjoy the destruction he created. He started the car, placed it in drive, and plowed from the graveled drive onto the asphalt paved road. As he drove from the engulfed inferno, screams of demons filled the air as the home dwindled in the cluster of amber and brick. The thick smoke floated through the air as it weighed upon the landscape like a thick black quilt that moved ever so slowly across the horizon.

Jonathan drove like a madman as he continued to his suite. He stayed fixed on Adrian and thought of various ways to kill him. His thoughts were abruptly shattered by the ring of his cell.

"What!" he shouted into the mouthpiece.

"I'm sorry, sir... I was calling to inform you that your father has planned for you to talk to the nations tomorrow, it is about the situation in Israel?"

Jonathan smiled. "Yes... yes, I almost forgot. I will be ready. What time is my flight?"

"You leave tomorrow at 9 a.m."

"Good, that leaves time for me and you... where are you now?"

"In your suite awaiting your command, sir."

"Good, I am on my way."

"Oh, and we do have company tonight. I invited some interns who are very eager to show their loyalty and undying support to you tonight."

Jonathan hung up the phone with a sly grin upon his face as he sped in anticipation to his suite, eager to greet his guests. Within minutes, he was met at the hotel and escorted to his suite. Jonathan dismissed his secret service men for the night and entered the suite.

Janice stood at the door eager to greet him; her sexy tone whispered in his ear, "They are ready."

Jonathan walked into the dimly lit room; it was adorned with strong-scented incense and candles. Pentagrams were strategically marked throughout the room as he gazed upon two ladies engaging in a steamy exchange of passionate kissing and fondling. Jonathan wasted no time as he undressed and positioned himself between the two interns. As they began to passionately kiss and fondle each other, an image of bodies protruded from within the walls as soft moans of people filled the air. One of the interns noticed the images and became afraid as she abruptly stopped and started to grab her clothes.

"That won't be necessary, dear," Janice stated as her facial complexion changed. Her teeth were multi-rowed as her completion turned demonic. She smiled as the intern's body was forced to the floor.

Jonathan smiled. "Now, Janice, is that any way to treat our guest?"

He let out a devilish cackle as screams of pain flood the walls of the room.

The Following Morning

Jonathan walked into the kitchen. It was 6:00 a.m., as he rubbed his head with the towel from the shower he had taken earlier. Janice was dressed and promptly waited to greet him with a cup of coffee and his itinerary.

"Good morning, sir, I hope last night was to your liking?"

"Yes, Janice, it was. Nice picks this time."

"I aim to please, sir. Here is your schedule for today. The council will be holding judgment proceeding against Senator Greenhouse today."

"Ahhh... Yes. I must attend that hearing today... Mr. Greenhouse will be an asset to today's activities. What else do I have?"

"You are scheduled to meet with the nations to declare war on the rebelling countries. Your father wishes to attend these proceedings as well."

"Good, Janice, and see that Mr. Greenhouse is flown to these proceedings also, we do need his cooperation on convincing the Joint Chiefs the importance of military involvement. Has the information been broadcasted?"

"See for yourself, sir," Janice exclaimed as she turned on the television.

"In other news, White House officials have determined that an Israeli radical group has claimed responsibility of the bombing of an ExxonMobile oil refinery. A reported 200 dead and 1,500 injured as firefighters and first responders tend to the injuries sustained."

Jonathan smiled. "This should be the fuel we need to bring Israel to its knees. Foolish insecure people will believe anything the media puts before them, and with revenge embedded in their hearts and minds, all they would want is retribution instead of truth. Yes, this will allow us to declare war on Israel with no problem. Well done, Janice, oh and by the way, the bodies?"

Janice smiled. "They were disposed of... I took the liberty to feast on one, I hope you don't mind, sir."

"Not at all, Janice, you deserve to have fun as well."

"Thank you, sir, I will have your suit out and ready for you. Your flight leaves at noon, and I will make arrangements to have Senator Greenhouse ready for boarding prior to departure. Is there anything else, sir?"

"Thank you, Janice, that will be all."

Jonathan sipped on his coffee and walked to the bedroom. He put on his suit and stared at himself in the mirror. Pleased with his appearance, he turned as Janice aided him with his tie.

"The car is ready out front. Will we be dining in the White House this evening, sir?"

"Yes, I have some guests meeting this evening. See that they are well taken care of."

"As you wish, sir. I will make the arrangements now," she replied as she walked alongside Jonathan.

Jonathan walked out of the hotel as several secret service men escorted him to The Beast. He thought that to be rather ironic to allow it to be named that under his administration. After a few security checks, the caravan was on their way. Within minutes, they arrived at Ellington Field. Jonathan boarded Air Force One, preceded by his secret service escorts, followed closely behind by Janice. All runways were cleared as Air Force One was cleared for takeoff. Janice met the president in the office room and briefly went over his itinerary once more as the secret service listened in. Everyone had to be on the same page to ensure the safety of the president.

Two hours later, Air Force One landed and the caravan was assembled once more. Jonathan and Janice were escorted to The Beast and within minutes whisked away to the White House. Jonathan and Janice were escorted to the congressional hearings as Jonathan walked into the room. Senator Greenhouse waited nervously. Upon seeing Jonathan, his demeanor turned from nervous to extremely cocky. Bickering proceeded back and forth between Greenhouse attorneys and the congressional panel. After a long bout, Jonathan interceded.

"Gentlemen, gentlemen. We all know of the alleged crimes of Senator Greenhouse. However, there is no sheer proof of him being involved. The crimes of assassination of the president and vice president are true acts of treason as we know to be punishable by death. My private investigative panel can show evidence that the assassination of the president and vice president was not done by the involvement of Senator Greenhouse, but was infiltrated by a domestic radical group involving the Arian Brotherhood of America whose sole purpose was to tumble the American government and reinstate Arian rule of the White House and take back their so-called 'true creed' of America."

The entire senate floor erupted into chaos and clatter as the House Speaker tried to maintain order.

Greenhouse smiled and shook his lawyer's hands in exuberance. He knew he was cleared.

Jonathan walked out of the proceedings and went to the oval office where he chuckled. Within minutes, the phone rang. Jonathan knew who it was as he picked up the phone.

"This is the president," he answered.

"How dare you betray us like that? We backed your campaign; we promoted your agenda. We acted upon your orders in the assassination and you know that. How dare you implement us in that! The NWO is the moral fiber of this country and—"

Jonathan interjected, "Shut the fuck up! Your radical organization promoted what we wanted it to promote—hate and despair. You stupid dust mongers have the audacity to ridicule your own kind for power, money, and political prestige. You were so focused on gaining your agenda and promoting your own ill-gotten purpose that you had no idea that you were doing the same thing you called yourself fighting against. You claim you are fighting to preserve morality within your country but still promoting hate... in GOD's name. You hypocritical bastards."

"You won't hear the last of this. We will expose you and what you stand for—"

Jonathan interrupted the caller, "Who do you think they will believe, me the savior of these United States who exposed the real plot behind the assassination of the president and vice president, or a bunch of red-necked, hillbilly wannabes who were too stupid to check the fine print?"

"Fine print? What fine print?"

"To trust no one." Jonathan hung up the phone. He leered at the phone and laughed.

Later That Afternoon

Jonathan had completed what he set out to do, which was to clear Greenhouse of all wrongdoing and bringing him in to aid in the swaying of the Joint Chiefs to declare war on Israel. They boarded Air Force One in silence. Janice escorted Jonathan and Greenhouse to the private office. She ordered the secret service to wait outside as she closed the door. Jonathan motioned for Greenhouse to sit. Jonathan grabbed a box from the table and retrieved a Cuban cigar. He politely offered one to his guest as he eagerly accepted the cigar. Jonathan snapped his finger as a controlled flame danced upon his fingertip; he lit his cigar and politely lit his guest's cigar. Greenhouse drew long deep puffs to get the flame to take effect on the tightly rolled tobacco.

"I can't believe you Americans would outlaw such a fine product," Jonathan exclaimed.

Greenhouse inhaled the rich smoke as he slowly exhaled the rich aroma through his nose. "Yes, it is a shame, isn't it?"

"So, Mr. Greenhouse, I have lived up to my end of the bargain, can we count on you to keep your end?"

"But of course, Mr. President. Even I know not to cross you."

"Well, Mr. Greenhouse. Now here is what I want you to do…"

There was a series of mumbles and whispers as the two talked. Janice excused herself from the room as she closed the door. She instructed the secret service that no one was to enter that room unless they cleared it with her first. They agreed as Janice walked away from the door into the coffee room. She poured herself a cup and hunkered down in the back cabin of the plane. She sipped her coffee as she examined the itinerary scheduled for the meeting with the nations.

Hours Later

Air Force One landed and the secret service men flooded the tarmac and cleared security for Jonathan and the senator to depart. They were hurried in The Beast and the caravan drove to the United Nations building. Minutes later they arrived.

The three exited the vehicle as secret service surrounded them. They walked into the building and proceeded to the conference as all the nations were present including the Joint Chiefs.

Jonathan took his place in his designated area at the table. Janice stood behind him eager to aid in any way possible. Senator Greenhouse joined the Joint Chiefs as he awaited his cue from Jonathan.

The country dignitaries argued among themselves as they wanted to prevent war with any country and wanted to resolve this issue by other means. Jonathan listened intently as they continued to argue. After what seemed to be forever, they finally addressed Jonathan.

"The room recognizes the United States."

Jonathan got to his feet and took his place at the podium.

"Distinguished guests. We are here to determine if actions are warranted against the terroristic attacks made by Israel. It is my understanding that the United States, although allied with this nation, had no involvement in its terroristic philosophy as they portrayed the façade of being a neutral country. With the recent events that took place this morning and the countless deaths that occurred due to the radical fundamentalist agenda that spurred this tragedy, we can no longer look to Israel as an allied nation, yet as a threat to our national security and well-being. The US by no means condone such actions, so effective immediately, we have placed government sanctions against Israel and have declared all military bases in and near Israel on high alert.

"With that, any threats incurred from this point on will mean a declared statement of war and will be received as such. Furthermore, we will retaliate against any and all threats and prove to Israel and any other nation that we will not bow to terror under any circumstances."

The entire building erupted in chaos as voices clamored amongst each other sounds of gaveling hit the wood with unpronounced force. Israel prime ministers were hurried out of the proceedings. The threat of war was in place.

That Evening

Jonathan walked into the formal dining room in the White House. He was eager to meet with his guests. Sitting before him was Lucifer, Vincent, and a few dignitaries. Jonathan smiled and nodded to his guests.

"Good evening, gentlemen. Glad you could make it. As you can see, the plan is in place. Senator Greenhouse has kept his end of the bargain by influencing the Joint Chiefs to strategically place military personnel in and around Israeli interests. It is only a matter of time that the once-formidable Israel will fall."

The dignitary from Egypt politely raised his hand to gain Jonathan's attention.

"Yes, Mr. Jehu Aksid."

"I applaud your accomplishments, Mr. President; however, would this not look bad against you and your administration once this war is implemented?"

Jonathan smiled and addressed the dignitary.

"Rest assured this will not look bad on my administration at all. It will actually allow me to be reelected. Gentlemen, this country in its present state is fueled by fear, fear of terrorism, fear of the mere change of their way of life. We use that fear to promote our agenda. That way revenge takes the place of reason, and no questions or doubts are ever surfaced. And when all else fails, well, Mr. Greenhouse took it upon himself to place this country in a war that would jeopardize the welfare of this nation and its government, hence the ultimate act of treason. And who is it that will run to the people's rescue?"

"You I assume?"

"But of course. Thus, furthering my agenda. I try Mr. Greenhouse for treason; look out for American interests by furthering the protection of our nation's interests and assuring the people the importance of winning this war. Deception, gentlemen, is the greatest thing to befall man; like I said before, trust no one, gentlemen."

The Long Journey

Adrian lolled on the plane anxious; he was filled with the adrenaline from the battle with Jonathan. The first encounter spoke volumes as to his matchup against the anti-Christ. He knew he could beat him. Titus must have read the cocky expression on his face because he shattered his fantasy and abruptly brought him back to reality.

"You only won because his minions surrounded him to protect him from you. You are strong but not strong enough to defeat him, not yet. I must admit you did well... very well in fact, but you are not strong enough... not yet."

Adrian veered at him in amazement. How could he know? Was he looking at his thoughts?

"How did you know what I was thinking?"

"I too was young once, you have the mind of a cocky teenager; you have that invincibility complex as most adolescent adults do, but mind you, his father is strong and will kill you."

Adrian eyed Titus and, without missing a beat, replied, "So is my father and he is much stronger, don't you agree?"

Titus smiled back. "Touché, Adrian... touché."

They both laughed as Adrian tended to Titus's wounds.

The shroud had completely healed the major wounds, and Titus was slowly regaining his strength. The flight to Amsterdam was long and unsettling as neither could rest comfortably. Ten hours later, they landed in Amsterdam. Adrian felt déjà vu as they debarked from the plane.

They mingled in with the small crowd as they walked to the baggage claim. Adrian kept a vigilant eye out for any suspicious characters that may want to hurt them. Luckily, no threats were in the area, and the two could get their belongings and exit the baggage area. Adrian hailed a cab and whisked himself and Titus in.

"Where to?" the cabbie asked.

Titus directed his attention toward the cab driver. "Amsterdam Suites."

Adrian smiled, seems he would be able to see his old friend James.

"We are going to see James?" Adrian asked.

"Yes, one, we would be safe there; second, James can give us the word as far as what Marek would want us to do next."

"It would be good to see James again."

Titus smiled. "I am certain he is looking forward to seeing you as well."

Amsterdam was cold and muggy for that time of the year. The glass on the car window fogged from the body heat generated from within. The lone dreary landscape scanned across the horizon like a pale vacant blanket, tattered with pale versions of unflattering patchwork feathered within the large landscape. They finally reached the familiar circular drive of the hotel. Adrian rushed out of the cab and grabbed the luggage. Almost as if on cue, James ran out to greet them.

"Hello, brother," James spoke and embraced Titus.

"Brother? You two are brothers?"

Titus smiled. "Yeah, this is my brother."

Adrian was in awe, but it explained a lot especially the battle in the alley. Adrian and Titus followed James into the hotel.

"I received word from Marek, you are to lay low here for a few weeks, but when called, Adrian, you must journey to Germany, there you must meet him for the next weapon you will be granted with. But until then, rest."

Adrian was looking forward to the next meeting with Marek; he could finally prove to Marek he could beat Satan, but at what cost?

A Few Weeks Later

Adrian woke to the sound of the television. The news of death and despair seemed to be an everyday norm in the broadcast. As he examined the area, he could notice the room seemed different. Adrian sat himself up in the bed and looked around the room again.

A voice spoke, "Adrian, you did well. It is not time for you to engage in battle yet. You will have an opportunity soon, but now you must continue to train. You must go back to Germany, as you will be trained more. You have done well, Adrian, and I admire your stand against Jonathan as well as the faith you have in your father. You will meet with Amelia, and she will take you to the safe house. Mind your promise to Tom and heed both of your safety because you will need to be vigilant on the company you address in the future."

Adrian nodded. "Who are you?"

The voice simply answered, "I am with you always, wherever I go, there ye shall be also."

Adrian felt at peace once again. He knew who that was. He lay back down and slept.

The next morning, Amelia came to the door and knocked several times.

"Adrian, we are ready, let's go."

"Are we not going to wait on Titus?"

Amelia shook her head no. "He and James both have business to attend prior to meeting us, but they will meet up with us soon. For now, we must be on our way."

Adrian grabbed his makeshift bag and followed Amelia to the cab waiting out front. Adrian continued his journey to his next stop, Germany. He must meet up with another angel—the name has not been revealed to him, but from the information relayed to him by Amelia from Titus, he will be revealed to him when the time comes. For now, he must venture forward. The trials are beginning; moments are even more critical than before. One thing can be said though; he did keep his promise to Tom, and Amelia was safe. Titus needed to heal; the battle took its toll on him. Adrian, however, was getting stronger and wiser than before.

He knew he had a long way to go and many more trials and tests to encounter, but one thing was certain, he would prevail against his foe, and he would win, for his sake, his family's, and for humanity's sake.

Chapter 8: Trouble Over the Horizon

The Third Seal

The mannerisms of the angry beast were unsettling, as the red horse snarled and bucked. Each stomp of its hoof created a loud thunder. The rage and eagerness glared from its cold black eyes. The rider looked up at GOD and laughed. Unlike Matthew, he looked forward to this day. He flashed a wicked smiled as the angels lined up on either side of him. The rider's air was cocky and intentional. His arrogance exuded as he mounted and commanded the reigns of the impatient beast. He manhandled the reigns as the beast resisted with all his might. The pull was so strong that blood oozed from the rider's hand when the rough leather dug deeper into his flesh. His uncanny laughter enraged the steed even more. The rider dominated the beast's head by forcefully tugging on the reigns. He signaled the seven angels, looked up at GOD one last time, before he began his ride.

The thunderous claps of the hooves boomed faster across the skies as the angry rider took his place as the prophecy had foretold. Sword wielded in-hand, his wicked laugh made even the angels cringe. The thunder of the hooves increased as he finally met up with his brothers Matthew and Marlon who looked back at him briefly in despair. The rider laughed even louder as he gazed upon his brother's dismay. Anger seethed through his cold black eyes. The heated mist resonated throughout the area. Marek's presence was revealed. The third seal had been broken.

Death Lurks from Within

A naval ship lay anchored patiently in the Mediterranean Sea. Sailors scurried along the deck preparing for battle. The Quarter Deck buzzed as the orders were relayed back and forth between the radioman and the officer of the deck.

"Sir, we have confirmation," the radioman stated as he tore off the printed orders from the White House.

"My God! This can't be happening..." The captain shuddered at the thought. He hurried the orders to the admiral who waited patiently in the war room.

"Sir, they have confirmed the orders we received earlier from the White House." The captain handed the paper to the admiral.

"May GOD forgive us for what we are about to do. Arm all missiles," barked the admiral hesitantly.

"Yes, sir, arming all missiles," the gunner shouted.

"On my mark; target bearing two zero, range three one four seven north, three five one three east, second mark three one point seven eight three north; bearing three five point two one seven east; ready, sir!"

The admiral looked at his watch and closed his eyes in dismay. "God forgive us," he prayed.

"FIRE!" the admiral shouted.

Four nuclear armed missiles sped toward its destination. The people unaware of the pending danger walked along the bustling streets of Jerusalem. Kids played among the cobblestoned streets as vendors and consumers exchanged tender and goods.

The missiles cued in on its projected target as cars scurried along its busy fairways.

Within seconds, the missiles reached their targets with extreme prejudice.

A large cloud billowed in the sky like a balloon mushroom that coated every inch of land with poison and radiation. Bodies were incinerated instantly. The buildings and structures tumbled like dominoes and were converted into dust and rubble.

The impact was felt by the ship that lay anchored out in the Mediterranean. Dead silence loomed aboard the ship. The evitable had been realized. The last war of the world began.

The phone rang several times before Jonathan rolled over and lifted the receiver from its cradle. He rubbed his eyes as he adjusted to the dimly lit room.

"Hello?"

"Mr. President. It is done."

"Good. Schedule a meeting with the press in the morning. We can negotiate the terms with Israel then."

"Yes, sir, Mr. President."

Jonathan hung up the phone and leaned over the side of the bed. He stood then walked over to the bathroom. He flipped the light switch on the marble-designed wall. He looked in the mirror and turned on the faucet as the water rushed uncontrollably. He splashed the cool liquid upon his face, its soothing mixture mixed with the dry flesh the night had endured upon him earlier.

A soft moan escaped from the bed as the covers made a soft scratching noise. The body exited the warm encasement.

Her soft pale white skin illuminated against dull man-made light as she entered into the bathroom.

"Why are you up so early?" Janice whispered.

"Seems the war has begun. Can you contact my father? We have a lot to discuss."

Janice kissed Jonathan softly on the lips. "As you wish, Mr. President." With that, she walked back into the bedroom.

Jonathan's lust-filled eyes followed behind her. He walked behind her and spun her around with animalistic force as he forced her back onto the bed. He parted her awaiting thighs and buried his head between them. She moaned in ecstasy as the sounds of moans and demonic screams circled the room.

Later That Morning

Cameras flashed violently against the empty podium. Multiple cameras clicked, and dull whispers echoed in the room as they impatiently awaited the emergence of the president.

Various reporters and cameramen scurried about in a chaotic orchestra vying for position to be able to get the first question. The word of the attack on Israel was leaked to the media and everyone wanted to know the reason.

There was a distinguished uniformed man that approached the podium. His dark blue uniform was adorned with gold stripes that jumped off the fabric. His chest was decorated with multiple ribbons and medals. His brass buttons glistened against the soft light occasionally adopting the flash of the camera bulbs as they exploded in the room. He laid some papers down and positioned the microphone ever so slightly. He glanced briefly at his notes and focused again on the reporters.

"Good morning. Thank you all for coming. Before I open the floor for questions, I would first like to address the reason for this conference. As most of you are aware, the recent bombing attack that took place last month on an ExxonMobil refinery that killed 200 employees and injured over 1,500. An investigation was launched in which Israeli fundamentalists that claimed responsibility for these attacks. Through failed governmental sanctions and resolve between US and Israeli officials, we've exhausted all measures to reach a diplomatic resolution. As of 9:00 a.m. Eastern Standard Time, in accordance to Congress, the United States has officially declared war on Israel. At 10:00 a.m. TLV/Israeli Daylight Time, 3:00 a.m. Eastern Standard Time, the USS *Brazos*, a nuclear armed battleship, fired four nuclear warhead missiles upon Jerusalem. Sources have confirmed that Jerusalem has been completely destroyed. We were led to this path due to failed governmental negotiations and orchestrated policies between the US and Israeli prime ministers." There was an eerier silence.

He took a deep breath, then continued. "Your questions will be answered, but I ask that you please wait until all officials address the media accordingly as to the events that brought us to this point. I now turn you over to the president of the United States."

Jonathan entered the room with elegance and grace as he stepped up to the podium. His expression was that of calm and content. He looked down at the podium for a brief second and gazed up at the cameras pointing at his dominating statue.

"I have approved of these attacks according to government regulations and protocol. The House and Senate approved by them as well. I wielded my right to use my executive order to pursue this objective with severe and extreme prejudice that the US will not wither nor will we falter. We will be forever vigilant in these trying times." He paused. "Israel, you have been notified through these actions that the US will continue to fight until the resolve has been achieved.

"For the fallen in the bombing of the ExxonMobil refinery, our sincere thoughts and prayers are with the families. I thank you and may GOD keep you and yours. May GOD bless you, and may he bless these United States of America."

Light bulbs flashed like lightning bolts. Reporters speaking over each other as voices chattered throughout the room. The president turned and walked away from the podium. The military official that spoke earlier returned to the podium began answering as many questions as he could without compromising national security. Jonathan began swelling inside with pride as he walked down the long corridor leading to the oval office. He motioned the secret service to stand outside as he entered the office.

Lucifer sat in the chair with his legs propped up on the desk. He was extremely elated as he witnessed his son walk through the door. "Well done, son! I've been wanting to destroy Jerusalem for centuries. Now let's see what that fuckin' Jesus has to say about things now." He chuckled.

"Thank you, Father, I knew you would approve. I have made arrangements with the Joint Chiefs to place strategic campaigns along the border to engage in retaliation against Israel and its allies."

Lucifer smiled. "Excellent. I already have Egypt, Afghanistan, and Iraq all on board to aid us in this fight. Bush and those other 'Bible-hugging' monkeys won't get onboard. The bastards were fighting the wrong enemy. We will win this war."

Jonathan joining in on his father's confidence agreed. "Yes, Father. We will."

Adrian woke up by a frantic knocking on the door. He looked at the clock on his nightstand. It read 3:00 a.m.

"Who in the hell?" he thought.

He positioned himself on the edge of the bed to allow the shock to diminish from the startling knock that woke him. The knocking continued as he stood and walked to the door with a hint of anger rushing his thoughts.

"Who is it?"

"Rashid, I have to speak to Titus now!" The voice boomed from the opposite side of the door.

By this time, Titus emerged from his room and instructed Adrian to open the door. A well-groomed middle-aged man eagerly entered the room. He looked to be 6'2" slender build. He appeared to be humble and modest in appearance.

"Asalam Alaikum, Titus."

"Wa Alaikum Asalam Wa Rahmatula, my friend. Adrian, this is my dear friend Ramon Aksid," Titus replied.

Adrian greeted Ramon with a handshake and motioned for him to sit in the living room.

"Titus, have you looked at the news this morning? The US just launched an attack on Israel. The prophecy has begun."

Titus looked to the floor in despair. The time had come and there was little time to lose. Adrian's preparation to lead came sooner than expected.

He turned to Adrian. "In my current state, I am unable to travel so you must go with Ramon. He will take you to a safe house. I will join you later. Heed Ramon's words well, Adrian, his knowledge will benefit you greatly. Ramon, say hello to our general, see that my friend is cared for and well prepared for battle."

Ramon shook Titus's hand. "By Allah's grace, he shall be ready."

Ramon's conversation was rushed and brief. "Hurry, Adrian, we don't have much time, and we have a lot to do before our trip to Megiddo."

Adrian looked puzzled. "But you're Muslim, I didn't think you believed in Christ."

Ramon smiled. "You Americans are all alike; brainwashed by your government believing all Muslims are the same, don't believe the prophet exists, warmongers, extreme terrorists, to know someone, you must first walk in his shoes; you will see you have more in common than you think."

Adrian felt bad from his comment, but Ramon sensing this reassured him it was okay. Adrian finished packing his bag. Before long, he was standing in the living room ready to leave with Ramon.

"Caution is no longer a luxury; Silas has begun his march with his act against Israel. It is time to fight with no mercy, no regrets. Listen and take heed to every word Ramon tells you. Your life will depend upon it. I will join you later. Now go."

Adrian and Ramon left and entered the elevator. Ramon escorted Adrian to a car waiting in front of the hotel entrance. Adrian thought to himself, *This is it, it's time.*

Chapter 9: Time to Put in Work

Ramon was not your ordinary Muslim, well, not in the sense of what ignorant Americans would consider Muslim. He cherished his body paying very close attention to what he placed in his body; he was devoted to his faith but not to a fault. He knew what his purpose was and the responsibilities he had vowed to uphold. Ramon eagerly rushed Adrian along.

"Hurry, my friend, we have a lot of ground to cover and a short time to do so." He led Adrian to a blue Mazda 7 parked out front. "Get in," he commanded. Ramon pressed the starter and the engine roared to life.

"You might want to buckle up... I tend to drive a little fast," Ramon warned.

Without warning, he punched the accelerator. Adrian was thrusted back in his seat with such force. Ramon realized what had happed and smiled. "Sorry 'bout that."

They traveled for hours talking about the events that had occurred over the past few hours. Adrian learned a lot from Ramon, things that had transpired and things that were to come.

"I am a member of a chapter known as the Templar of Knights. We were created after the Last Crusades in 1272. We had taken possession of the Arc of the Covenant four years earlier and taken it to a temple we had established in Ethiopia. During World War 2, when Mussolini vowed to attack Ethiopia, we moved the arc to a safe haven in Poland where a British intelligence group was able to get it safely to a ship bound for the US where it has been since."

Adrian was confused. "I thought the Templar of Knights were a Christian group?"

"You Americans and your trust in history. The Templar consisted of both Muslim and Christian alike. When Silas learned of the Arc and its location, he turned a few of the templars against one another which caused chaos among our ranks. With this seed placed in the ranks, trust was dissolved to the point where Muslim involvement was frowned upon. Those who stayed true to the creed broke off and went underground. Where we remained for centuries."

"So why are you emerging now? Aren't you afraid of retaliation from the defectors?" Adrian asked.

"No."

"Why not?" Adrian asked.

"Because we are needed. And I vowed to give my life for my fellow man regardless of the religious belief, racial persuasion, or governmental ideology. When it is all said and done, it is Allah's will. Don't you agree?"

Adrian could not argue with him on that note. "We are all created in his image... ," Adrian added.

"Precisely, my friend, precisely."

Megiddo—the roads looked desolate and baron. The deserts back home looked nothing like this. Nothing as far as the eye can see and it was hot—too hot. They drove to a stone temple alongside of a large hill. Ramon pulled the car in front of the temple and placed the vehicle in park. He turned off the engine.

"We have arrived. Come we have a lot to do. Also, there is someone you must meet," Ramon ordered.

Adrian exited the car when a man in a Thobe greeted him. The long black material moved gracefully as he greeted Adrian.

"Good to finally meet the prophecy. I am Aakifah, come, I will show you to your quarters."

They walked inside the temple; candles dimly lit the walkway leading to the grand room. Within the grand room were torches and a small group of men gathered around a large table. They were of all races and nationalities. Adrian was shocked. Engraved in the middle of the table were the markings of the twelve tribes of Israel. As Adrian approached, the room grew silent as the men at the table stood. The person at the head of the table smiled and walked around to greet Adrian.

"Welcome, my son. Your presence was foretold to us. Come, let's get you settled. There is much work to be done and your training must begin soon."

"I'm sorry not trying to be rude but... who are you, and what is this place?" Adrian asked.

"You wouldn't believe me if I told you, my son," the man answered.

"Try me."

"I am Lazarus, brother of Mary Magdalene."

"You are right, I don't believe you," Adrian exclaimed.

Lazarus laughed. "Come."

Later that evening, Lazarus, Adrian, and Ramon sat at the grand table discussing the things that had transpired thus far.

"Jonathan has gotten stronger, more brash in his methods of attack. He has more political backing not only in the US but among many nations that are against Israel. This was the plan all along. It was inevitable. Israel must fall in order for the battle to take place," Lazarus explained.

"Wow, those Sunday school class seemed to come in handy now... glad I went to church," Adrian joked.

"As humorous as that was, my friend, there were much that was left out of your teachings. Megiddo is only the beginning. The Townsend brothers have all began their rides except one. And I am afraid he will begin his ride here very soon, which does not leave us much time to prepare," Lazarus exclaimed.

"With that said, you may want to get some rest, my friend, we have a busy day tomorrow and you will need all your strength to make it through... at least to lunch."

"Great, another Marek..." Adrian shook his head.

"Marek is a lightweight... I am much worse," Ramon boasted.

"Damn, damn, damn!" Adrian mumbled.

Adrian was escorted to his quarters; as he entered the room he was assigned, he noticed its simplicity. Oh, how he missed the Amsterdam Waldorf Astoria! There was a simple twin bed rested neatly against a clay-colored wall, on either side a makeshift nightstand devised of two crate-like tables. There was one chair and a large crate that was used as a table. A small generator-type engine sat in a corner near an open shuttered window. Not the best accommodations, but it was home for now, Adrian thought.

"Yes, it is our version of the Waldorf Astoria Amsterdam, Adrian!" Ramon laughed. "Sleep, we will begin training in the morning."

"How in the hell..." Adrian turned to ask Ramon how did he know what he was thinking, but before he could, Ramon had departed. Baffled, Adrian shrugged it off and prepared for bed.

The Dream

Adrian woke from his slumber. Sleep seemed to cloud his eyes like a muddled fog. He remained motionless for a few moments to gain his sight. He turned over to notice his wife, Stephanie, still asleep. Her angelic profile looked peaceful and content. He leaned over and slightly and gently gave a soft peck on the cheek. He made every effort to exit the bed without waking her as he slipped on his makeshift slippers. He carefully eased off of the bedroom.

He covered her up with the blanket she had pushed off her and walked out of the room pulling the door shut behind him. He made his way to Alice's room. She was true to form, she was almost out of bed. Her little legs struggling to balance between the mattress and the floor. Adrian chuckled; he picked her up and arranged her correctly in her bed, covered her up with the blanket, and kissed her little forehead. She tooted her butt in the air and let out three muffled farts. Yeah, she was true to form. Adrian walked downstairs to the kitchen, grabbed a drink of water, and turned on the television downstairs. As the screen flickered on, he could hear a voice. "You can have this back you know. Your family alive and well."

Adrian looked around. "Who is there? How did you get in my house?"

"Come now, you know good and damn well who I am, and you know this is not your house. But let's not be so technical here, shall we?"

"Adrian, what's happening? Adrian! No, Adrian, don't let go please, Adrian. No... no, please, Adrian!"

His daughter's screams could be heard in the background as they pleaded for him to save them.

"Daddy, please help me, I am afraid of him!" Sarah screamed.

Then there was another shriek as Faith begged for her daddy to help her. "Daddy, he is here, I see him, Daddy, please help me, Daddy... Daddy!"

Adrian screamed for his family as the room continued to get dark. He could not find them as the closer he ran to their voice, the more distant they became. A voice echoed in the darkness.

"Leave them alone, you son of a bitch!"

"OH, such language, please, do you kiss your mother with that mouth? I am certain you don't use that language in front of your kids."

Adrian could hear the screams from the girls. "Daddy, please help, it is dark in here. They are trying to get me!" Samantha screamed.

Alice screamed a bloodcurdling scream, "Daddy! Daddy! Help me please... DADDY!"

"Leave them alone, I said!" Adrian screamed.

"Why, of course, as soon as you give up this little tiff of a crusade. Come to me, serve me, and you can have your heart's desire."

"You would rather rule in hell than to serve in heaven, am I right?"

"The benefits seem to be better, I must say. And besides to serve a sanicle God like that... it is the ultimate insult."

"Fuck you, Silas... Yeah, I know who you are... who you really are!"

"Anger; I like that... that's good... feed into that anger, the hatred you have inside of you. Let it build; this will be your strength, your fuel to conquer. Let it build in you."

Adrian felt the anger build inside of him, the anguish and despair of his family, the lack of his ability to save them rushed through his thoughts as if to play a cruel and thoughtless trick to his soul. Adrian wanted to give in to the anger, the hatred, the despair, but something within him made him chose different.

"I will not give in to your temptation, I know not all men are evil, I will hold fast to GOD's mercy; you will not have me."

"GOD? You call that bastard a GOD; he took your family from you! You stupid fucker! You still want to worship a sadistic son of a bitch like that? I can give you your family back; damn GOD and follow me!"

"No, I WILL STAND FAST! GOD WILL KEEP ME AND PROTECT ME! TO HELL WITH YOU; YOU SON OF A BITCH!"

"You will be mine, Adrian, this I vow." The voice cackled wickedly.

Adrian's blood boiled, but he thought about it and calmed instead.

"I'm like Stevie Wonder, I can't see joining you, Silas. Free will is the choice us humans possess, and it is ultimately up to us to choose what is right and wrong for our lives... and frankly... I don't think you are right for me, not now, not ever. So as we say in the hood... poof be gone, muthafucker."

Silas screamed, "NO! You will turn this, I promise you."

"I wish a nigga would," Adrian replied.

And with that, he sat up in his bed. He was somewhat shaken that Silas could reach him from so far away. How was he able to get to him? He sat awake for a moment, pondering the dream he had just had. He looked at his phone, two thirty in the morning. He turned over still thinking about what happened afraid to return to the dream but eager to confront Silas once again. Unfortunately, as he drifted back to sleep, he was given that opportunity again.

Adrian was awakened by Ramon. He explained the dream to him in great detail. Once Adrian was done, Ramon looked at him in shock.

"You have been around Marek too long. Your ghetto vernacular is very funny. Come, let's tell Lazarus of your dream... but without the extras."

Adrian laughed. "Agreed. But I am curious how was he able to reach me..."

Ramon explained, "The dreams are open realms to the spirit world, easy to access, it allows communication with the dead as well as your subconscious. It would not be very difficult for him to reach you there. It is of no major concern, but I think it be best to inform Lazarus anyway."

Adrian agreed and followed Ramon to Lazarus's quarters. After explaining the dream, Lazarus chuckled.

"He is desperate. That is good, lets me know he is letting his guard down. Let me worry about this; right now, you have training, do you not?"

Ramon smiled. "That's me, I'm up."

Ramon had Adrian follow him to an outdoor arena. Out in the courtyard stood a stand with swords, spears, maces, and knives of various sorts.

"Aww... no guns?" Adrian joked.

Ramon smiled. "Conventional soldiers use such weaponry... however, we are not conventional."

Ramon grabbed two swords and threw one at Arian; he caught it in midair.

"Attack me!" Ramon commanded.

Adrian lunged at Ramon as he sidestepped Adrian and pushed him to the ground.

"Your enemy will not fight with honor, remember, these are demons' minions of Silas; honor is not in his vocabulary. Again."

Adrian calculated his move before attempting to strike Ramon again; he lunged at him once more, did a quick turn to hit Ramon from the back, but Ramon countered and, with a force from his hand, repelled Adrian's body across the courtyard.

"Hey, that kinda hurt!" Adrian exclaimed as he slowly pulled himself off the ground. The impact sore and tender, he nursed it as much as he could by rubbing it—to no avail, of course.

"Use all the talents given unto you, never limit yourself to one attack. Trust me, they will not. They will do whatever necessary to ensure you do not live to see the end of this journey, this you must always remember."

Adrian listened intently. He thought to himself, "He was right, he is worse than Marek when it comes to training... Hell, that hurt!"

"I am glad now maybe you will appreciate the urgency of this training," a voice answered back.

Adrian stopped. "What the hell... were you reading my mind or something?"

Ramon stopped. "Yes, as will they. They will try and distract you using every effort of controlling your emotions, your very soul. You must be as strong mentally as you are physically. Otherwise, all the physical strength in the world would not save you. Again!"

They trained well into the afternoon stopping only to eat. Adrian learned a lot from Ramon and some interesting history about his past as well.

They sat in the courtyard as they feasted upon fruit, dried meat, and a bread loaf.

"I was raised here by my father; my mother was killed by Silas when I was about three. He tried to turn my dad, but my dad refused, so he figured he would take away what he loved the most... my mother and I. Lazarus came and retrieved me, brought me here to live."

"And your father? What happened to him?" Adrian asked.

"Sadly, my dad died in battle, he was killed by Silas in the states. I swore I would train day and night to get my revenge... I will fight until I have no breath left."

Adrian and Ramon sat in silence for a brief moment. Afterward, Adrian opened up about his family tragedy. Ramon listened intently. Upon Adrian's conclusion, he looked at Adrian with compassion and concern. "Use that to help you fight, but never let it consume you. Anger poisons the mind and dulls the reflexes. Use that emotion to strengthen you, allow it to be your purpose to succeed."

Adrian nodded his head in confirmation. They continued to eat in silence.

Aakifah walked up to the two men, found a spot, and sat down.

"Hello, Adrian, it is time you start strengthening your mind, my friend."

Ramon nodded at Aakifah and stood to depart as he turned around to warn Adrian. "You think I'm bad... you need to watch this guy."

Adrian looked at him in shock. *What the hell have I gotten into*? he thought.

Not hell, Adrian, but it will feel like it once we are through, a voice beckoned in his head.

"As I stated earlier, we are going to strengthen your mind. Demons are famous for mind play; they use your deepest fears to weaken you mentally which will rob you physically. Your job is to fight this attack."

Aakifah stared at Adrian; he reached into the bare essence of his thoughts, pulling away from it the death of his family. Adrian tried to block him but was unsuccessful.

"Use it! Use this memory to counter."

Adrian yelled, "I don't know how!"

Aakifah stopped. "It's okay, my friend, after I am done with you, you will."

Adrian and Aakifah trained well into the evening strengthening his mind by mastering his emotions, focusing on his concentration. Mentally Adrian was drained, but he refused to give in as he continued to improve with each lesson.

It was near dark when Aakifah stopped his training. "Well done, Adrian; come let's eat, you will need your strength for tomorrow's training."

Adrian was exhausted and hungry. He was pleased at the strives he had made over the day and was eagerly looking forward to tomorrow's training. They met in a dining hall where there was a large group of people feasting and conversating. Adrian sat next to Ramon and Aakifah. They ate and conversed for some time. Mulling over the day's training and analyzing improvements, Adrian needed to focus on in the future. Before long, they broke to retire for the night. Adrian went back to his quarters. Pleased with his progress, he sat on the side of the bed and smiled. He picked up his cell phone from the side of the makeshift nightstand and scrolled through his family pictures. He put his phone back on the table and laid down on the bed. Within minutes, he was fast asleep.

Chapter 10: Titus's Descent–Virginia 1762

Titus looked at his arms and legs; shackled, he was attached to a line of others in the same bondage. Skins of different hues collectively lined up before him limited by movement as they were instructed to move ahead. They were placed on a wooden platform. A man walked among each slave as he examined the teeth, arms, legs, as if inspecting an animal. He grunted and instructed on which ones he was purchasing. There was another man with a ledger scribbling information inside. Shortly they were instructed to move from the platform back to the ground below. The dirt was rough and coarse to the soles of his feet. The smell of must and sweat engulfed his nostrils almost overpowering his senses. They walked behind a horse-drawn wagon for what seemed like forever stopping briefly for a sip of water and a moment's rest. Finally, arriving to their destination, they were placed in a barn where other slaves tended to them to prepare them for their destined new life—slave labor.

Months Later

The days seemed to get worse for Titus; the days were long, tiring. "How can men treat their brothers in such a manner?" he thought.

While working, a small and gentle hand touched his. He looked up from his labor to notice a beautiful young woman gazing back at him. Her soft complexion was slightly stained with pain and anguish. He smiled as she dipped her ladle in the water bucket. She gracefully handed him the ladle, and he graciously accepted it. He drank the water, its warm but soothing form coated his dry and parched throat, providing temporary relief.

"Move on, girl!" the overseer shouted.

Titus wanted to know her name, but before he could ask, she volunteered.

"Elizabeth. They's call me Lizzie."

Titus smiled. "Lizzie."

Titus got to know Lizzie overtime, sneaking off to meet whenever possible. They grew very fond of each other. Titus never knew love, not in the physical sense. He felt he could not allow any harm to come to her. This was a feeling he really enjoyed. To care for someone other than self to the point you would be willing to give your life for. It was a repeat of the months before, hot, sweaty, long, and grueling. Lizzie made her regular rounds of providing water during their brief breaks.

"Meet me tonight, Lizzie," Titus whispered.

"K, I's will. Come to the woodshed after midnight." She gave a sly smile and looked to the ground as to not draw suspicion from the overseer.

Titus smiled. He went back to work as Lizzie walked away with a smile she could not contain.

Night came as Titus waited till the moon sat high in the sky, this was his indication of time. He rose from his dirt-stained pallet cushioned only by loose straw from the barn from where he would refresh from time to time. He opened the door and looked outside to make sure no one was around. He rushed across the plantation toward the woodshed. Prior to arriving, he heard rustling.

"Come here, gal," a voice said in a low tone.

Titus stopped and hid behind a buggy parked nearby. The overseer threw Lizzie to the ground; her dress was torn and tattered. He unbuckled his pants and pulled them down, he pounced upon Lizzie like a wild animal, pulling her dress up; he proceeded to penetrate her, he muffled her mouth so as to prevent her from screaming. Titus's eyes grew dark, the skies turned black as a dark silk cloth.

The overseer raised up from Lizzie, his body trembled, and shortly, he collapsed.

Lizzie scurried back away from the lifeless body.

Titus ran toward Lizzie.

"It's okay, Lizzie. Come, we must leave."

He escorted Lizzie back to his hut. "What happened to Mista Turner. I's never seen such a thing before. It got so dark... like death!" Lizzie exclaimed.

Titus held her tight to comfort her. She was frightened, but his embrace was comforting. Titus closed his eyes and placed his hand on her forehead. Within seconds, she was sleep. He lay her down on his pallet. He thought about what he did but was remorseful only for a few moments. He lay next to her and drifted to sleep.

Titus was awakened by shouting and yelling, he looked around, Lizzie had gone. He went outside to see the slaves gathered around. No one was saying a word.

"Seems like the old fella had a heart attack I suppose," the doctor stated.

The plantation owner scratched his head. "Get these niggas back to work; send word to his family. Cyrus, get the body on the buggy and get him to the family for burial."

"Yes, sir," Cyrus replied.

Titus and Lizzie's relationship blossomed over time and soon Titus and Lizzie jumped the broom. A few years later, she gave birth to a son, to whom he named Daniel. They were happy considering the situation, but Titus wanted to be free. He wanted his family free.

England 1875

Titus sat in the parlor of his friends' home. He sipped on a smooth brandy looking at documents sent to him from the states. It was almost a decade since the end of the Civil War. Titus looked at the documents that lay before him.

They were the freedom papers sent to him of his son and wife. A tear ran down his cheek as he sipped his brandy once more. All these years and he still remembered it as if it were yesterday.

"Are you okay, my friend?" James Gresham asked.

"I am well, my brother."

James smiled. "Don't grieve, my friend, you will see them again soon."

Titus found comfort in that statement. He shook his head in agreement and sipped his brandy.

Present Day

Titus drove to the temple in Megiddo. He pulled in front and placed the car in park. He exited the car and was greeted by Aakifah.

"You have gotten rather comfortable reading people's thoughts," Titus exclaimed.

"Forgive me, Titus, I meant no harm."

"No need for apologies, Aakifah. I meant that in a respectful way, trust me, no harm done."

"You miss your family... I understand, Titus."

Titus smiled. "I know you do. Where is Lazarus? I speak with him."

Aakifah escorted Titus to Lazarus. Aakifah excused himself as he left the two to talk.

"Greetings, ole friend." Lazarus embraced him.

"It has been a while, how is the recruit coming along?"

"He is progressing rather swiftly. His resolve is like nothing I have ever encountered. He reminds me of you, my friend."

"Yes, I would have to agree," Titus stated.

Lazarus motioned Titus in a small room. A makeshift table made of a cargo crate sat neatly centered in the room. Upon it sat a small teapot with two cups. "Sit, my friend."

The two men sat at the table as Lazarus poured tea in each cup. "You look troubled, my friend."

"Yes, I am worried about Amelia, she is smart and scrappy, but this task is too dangerous for her."

Lazarus shook his head in agreement. "That she is, but she posses the gift of sight the gift bestowed upon Joseph. Her ability to decipher the scroll is invaluable."

"Yes, I know; that is why I am even more concerned. We are placing her life in danger," Titus stated.

"We will provide every measure to keep her safe."

"I know, that is why I must guard her. I must keep her close at all times. Marek will be here within the week with her and the scroll. How is the arc—"

"It is safe, my friend, don't worry." Lazarus comforted his friend.

Titus knew this was going to be the end of his journey. He just felt it.